Puffin Books

THE Wave

Laurie isn't sure what to make of 'The Wave'. It had begun as a simple history experiment to liven up their World War II studies and had become a fad that was taking over their lives. 'The Wave' was sweeping through the school – and it was out of control.

Laurie's friends scoff at her warnings but she knows she must make them see what they have become before it's too late.

This chilling novel, based on a nightmarish true episode in a Californian high school, shows just how easily a group can lose its freedom without even realizing it.

31

MORTON RHUE

THE Wave

PUFFIN BOOKS

PUFFIN BOOKS

Published by the Penguin Group
Penguin Books Ltd, 80 Strand, London WC2R 0RL, England
Penguin Putnam Inc., 375 Hudson Street, New York, New York 10014, USA
Penguin Books Australia Ltd, Ringwood, Victoria, Australia
Penguin Books Canada Ltd, 10 Alcorn Avenue, Toronto, Ontario, Canada M4V 3B2
Penguin Books India (P) Ltd, 11 Community Centre, Panchsheel Park, New Delhi – 110 017, India
Penguin Books (NZ) Ltd, Cnr Rosedale and Airborne Roads, Albany, Auckland, New Zealand
Penguin Books (South Africa) (Pty) Ltd, 24 Sturdee Avenue, Rosebank 2196 South Africa

Penguin Books Ltd, Registered Offices: 80 Strand, London WC2R 0RL, England

www.penguin.com

This work is a novelization of a teleplay by Johnny Dawkins
based on a short story by Ron Jones.
Published by arrangement with Dell Publishing Co., Inc., New York.

First published in the USA by Dell Publishing Co., Inc. 1981
First published in Great Britain by Puffin Books 1982
Published simultaneously in hardback by Kestrel Books
Reprinted in Penguin Books 1988
Reissued in Puffin Books 1994

15

Text copyright © Dell Publishing Co., Inc.
and TAT Communications Company, 1981
Cover photo copyright © TAT Communications Company, 1981
All rights reserved

Printed in England by Clays Ltd, St Ives plc
Filmset in Monophoto Ehrhardt

Contents

Chapter One

Laurie Saunders sat in the publications office at Gordon High School chewing on the end of a Bic pen. She was a pretty girl with short light-brown hair and an almost perpetual smile that only disappeared when she was upset or chewing on Bic pens. Lately she'd been chewing on a lot of pens. In fact, there wasn't a single pen or pencil in her pocket-book that wasn't worn down on the butt end from nervous gnawing. Still, it beat smoking.

Laurie looked around the small office, a room filled with desks, typewriters, and light tables. At that moment there should have been kids at each one of those typewriters, punching out stories for *The Gordon Grapevine*, the school paper. The art and layout staff should have been working at the light tables, laying out the next issue. But instead the room was empty except for Laurie. The problem was that it was a beautiful day outside.

Laurie felt the plastic tube of the pen crack. Her mother had warned her once that someday she would chew on a pen until it splintered and a long plastic shard would lodge in her throat and she would choke to death on it. Only her mother could have come up with that, Laurie thought with a sigh.

She looked up at the clock on the wall. Only a few minutes were left in the period anyway. There was no rule that said anyone had to work in the publications office during their free periods, but they all knew that the next edition of *The Grapevine* was due out next week. Couldn't they give up their Frisbees and cigarettes and suntans for just a few days in order to get an issue of the paper out on time?

7

Laurie put her pen back in her pocket-book and started to gather up her notebooks for the next period. It was hopeless. For the three years she'd been on the staff, *The Grapevine* had always been late. And now that she was the editor-in-chief it made no difference. The paper would be done when everyone got around to doing it.

Pulling the door of the publications office closed behind her, Laurie stepped out into the hall. It was practically empty now; the bell to change classes had not yet rung, and there were only a few students around. Laurie walked down a few doors, stopped outside a classroom, and peered through the window.

Inside, her best friend, Amy Smith, a petite girl with thick, curly, Goldilocks hair, was trying to endure the final moments of Mr Gabondi's French class. Laurie had taken French with Mr Gabondi the year before and it had been one of the most ex-cruciatingly boring experiences of her life. Mr Gabondi was a short, dark, heavy-set man who always seemed to be sweating, even on the coldest winter days. When he taught, he spoke in a dull monotone that could easily put the brightest student to sleep, and even though the course he taught was not difficult, Laurie recalled how hard it had been to pay enough attention to get an *A*.

Now watching her friend struggle to stay interested, Laurie decided she needed some cheering up. So, positioning herself outside the door where Amy could see her but Gabondi could not, Laurie crossed her eyes and made an idiotic face. Amy reacted by putting her hand over her mouth to keep from laughing. Laurie made another face and Amy tried not to look, but she couldn't help turning back to see what her friend was doing next. Then Laurie did her famous fish face: she pushed her ears out, crossed her eyes, and puckered her lips. Amy was trying so hard not to laugh that tears started to roll down her cheeks.

Laurie knew she shouldn't make any more faces. Watching Amy was too funny – anything could make her laugh. If Laurie did any more, Amy would probably fall out of her seat and roll into the aisle between the desks. But Laurie couldn't resist. Turning her back to the door to create some suspense, she screwed up her mouth and eyes, and then spun around.

8

Standing at the door was a very angry Mr Gabondi. Behind him Amy and the rest of her class were in hysterics. Laurie's jaw dropped. But before Gabondi could reprimand her, the bell rang and his class was suddenly spilling out into the hall around him. Amy came out holding her sides in pain from laughing so hard. As Mr Gabondi glared at them, the two girls went off arm in arm towards their next class, too out of breath to laugh any more.

In the classroom where he taught history, Ben Ross crouched over a film projector, trying to thread a film through the complex maze of rollers and lenses. This was his fourth attempt and he still hadn't got it right. Frustrated, Ben ran his fingers through his wavy brown hair. All his life he had been befuddled by machinery – film projectors, cars, even the self-service pump at the local garage drove him bananas.

He had never been able to figure out why he was so inept in that way, and so when it came to anything mechanical, he left it to Christy, his wife. She taught music and choir at Gordon High, and at home she was in charge of anything that required manual dexterity. She often joked that Ben couldn't even be trusted to change a light bulb correctly, although Ben insisted this was an exaggeration. He had changed a number of light bulbs in his life and could only recall breaking two in the process.

Thus far in his career at Gordon High – Ben and Christy had been teaching there for two years – he had managed to hide his mechanical inabilities. Or rather, they had been overshadowed by his growing reputation as an outstanding young teacher. Ben's students spoke of his intensity – the way he got so interested and involved in a topic that they couldn't help but be interested also. He was 'contagious', they'd say, meaning that he was charismatic. He could get through to them.

Ross's fellow faculty members were somewhat more divided in their feelings towards him. Some of them were impressed with his energy and dedication and creativity. It was said that he brought a new outlook to his classes, that, whenever possible, he tried to teach his students the practical, relevant aspects of history. If they were studying the political system, he would divide the class into political parties. If they studied a famous trial, he might assign one student to be the defendant, others to be the prosecution and defence lawyers, and still others to sit as the jury.

But other faculty members were more sceptical about Ben. Some said he was just young, naïve, and over-zealous, that after a few years he would calm down and start conducting classes the 'right' way – lots of reading, weekly quizzes, classroom lectures. Others simply said they didn't like the way he never wore a suit and tie in class. One or two might even admit they were just plain jealous.

But if there was one thing no teacher had to be jealous of, it was Ben's total inability to cope with film projectors. While perhaps brilliant otherwise, now he only scratched his head and looked at the tangle of celluloid bunched in the machine. In just a few minutes his senior history class would arrive, and he had been looking forward to showing them this film for weeks. Why hadn't his teacher's college given a course in film threading?

Ross rolled the film back into its spool and left it unthreaded. No doubt one of the kids in his class was some kind of audiovisual whiz and could get the machine going in an instant. He walked back to his desk and picked up a pile of homework papers he wanted to distribute to the students before they saw the film.

The marks on the papers had become predictable, Ben thought as he thumbed through them. As usual, there were two *A* papers, Laurie Saunders's and Amy Smith's. There was one *A* − , then the normal bunch of *B*'s and *C*'s. There were two *D*'s. One was Brian Ammon, a quarterback on the football team, who seemed to enjoy getting low marks, even though it was obvious to Ben that he had the brains to do much better if he tried. The other *D* was Robert Billings, the class loser. Ross shook his head. The Billings boy was a real problem.

Outside in the hall the bells rang, and Ben heard the sounds of class doors banging open and students flooding into the corridors. It was peculiar how students always left class so quickly but some-how arrived at their next class at the speed of snails. Generally Ben believed that high school today was a better place for kids to learn than it was when he went. But there were a few things that bothered him. One was his students' lackadaisical attitude about getting to class on time. Sometimes five or even ten minutes of valuable class time would be lost while students straggled in. Back when he was a student, if you weren't in class when the second bell rang, you were in trouble.

The other problem was the homework. Kids just didn't feel compelled to do it any more. You could yell, threaten them with *F*'s or detention, and it didn't matter. Homework had become practically optional. Or, as one of his ninth-graders had told him a few weeks before, 'Sure I know homework is important, Mr Ross, but my social life comes first.'

Ben chuckled. Social life.

Students were starting to enter the classroom now. Ross spotted David Collins, a tall, good-looking boy who was a running back on the football team. He was also Laurie Saunders's boyfriend.

'David,' Ross said, 'do you think you could get that film projector set up?'

'Sure thing,' David replied.

As Ross watched, David kneeled beside the projector and went to work nimbly. In just a few seconds he had it threaded. Ben smiled and thanked him.

Robert Billings trudged into the room. He was a heavy boy with shirt-tails perpetually hanging out and his hair always a mess, as if he never bothered to comb it after getting out of bed in the morning. 'We gonna see a movie?' he asked when he saw the projector.

'No, dummy,' said a boy named Brad, who especially enjoyed tormenting him. 'Mr Ross just likes to set up projectors for fun.'

'Okay, Brad,' Ben said sternly. 'That's enough.'

A sufficient number of students had arrived for Ross to start handing out the homework papers. 'All right,' he said loudly to get the class's attention. 'Here are last week's papers. Generally speaking, you did a good job.' He walked up and down the aisles passing each paper to its author. 'But I'm warning you again. These papers are getting much too sloppy.' He stopped and held one up for the class to see. 'Look at this. Is it really necessary to doodle in the margins of a homework paper?'

The class tittered. 'Whose is it?' someone asked.

'None of your business.' Ben shuffled the papers in his hand and kept handing them out. 'From now on, I'm going to start lowering grades on any papers that are really sloppy. If you've made a lot of changes or mistakes on a paper, make a new, neat copy before you hand it in. Got that?'

Some members of the class nodded. Others weren't even paying attention. Ben went to the front of the classroom and pulled down the movie screen. It was the third time that semester he'd talked to them about messy homework.

Chapter Two

They were studying World War Two, and the film Ben Ross was showing his class that day was a documentary depicting the atrocities the Nazis committed in their concentration camps. In the darkened classroom the class stared at the movie screen. They saw emaciated men and women starved so severely that they appeared to be nothing more than skeletons covered with skin. People whose knee joints were the widest parts of their legs.

Ben had already seen this film or films like it half a dozen times. But the sight of such ruthless inhumane cruelty by the Nazis still horrified him and made him feel angry. As the film rolled on, he spoke emotionally to the class: 'What you are watching took place in Germany between 1934 and 1945. It was the work of a man named Adolf Hitler, originally a menial labourer, porter, and house painter, who turned to politics after World War One. Germany had been defeated in that war, its leadership was at a low ebb, inflation was high, and thousands were homeless, hungry, and jobless.

'For Hitler it was an opportunity to rise quickly through the political ranks of the Nazi Party. He espoused the theory that the Jews were the destroyers of civilization and that the Germans were a superior race. Today we know that Hitler was a paranoid, a psychopath, literally a madman. In 1923 he was thrown in jail for his political activities, but by 1934 he and his party had seized control of the German government.'

Ben paused for a moment to let the students watch more of the film. They could see the gas chambers now, and the piles of bodies laid out like stove wood. The human skeletons still alive had the gruesome task of stacking the dead under the watching eyes of the Nazi soldiers. Ben felt his stomach churn. How on God's earth could anyone make anyone else do something like that, he asked himself.

He told the students: 'The death camps were what Hitler called his "Final solution to the Jewish problem". But anyone – not just Jews – deemed by the Nazis as unfit for their superior race was sent there. They were herded into camps all over Eastern Europe, and once there they were worked, starved, and tortured, and when they couldn't work any more, they were exterminated in the gas chambers. Their remains were disposed of in ovens.' Ben paused for a moment and then added: 'The life expectancy of the prisoners in the camps was two hundred and seventy days. But many did not survive a week.'

On the screen they could see the buildings that housed the ovens. Ben thought of telling the students that the smoke rising from the chimneys above the buildings was from burning human flesh. But he didn't. The experience of watching this film would be awful enough. Thank God man had not invented a way to convey smells through film, because the worst thing of all would have been the stench of it, the stench of the most heinous act ever committed in the history of the human race.

The film was ending and Ben told his students: 'In all, the Nazis murdered more than ten million men, women, and children in their extermination camps.'

The film was over. A student near the door flicked the classroom lights on. As Ben looked around the room, most of the students looked stunned. Ben had not meant to shock them, but he'd known that the film would. Most of these students had grown up in the small, suburban community that spread out lazily around Gordon High. They were the products of stable, middle-class families, and despite the violence-saturated media that permeated society around them, they were surprisingly naïve and sheltered. Even now a few of the students were starting to fool around. The misery and horror depicted in the film must have seemed to them like just another television programme. Robert Billings, sitting near the windows, was asleep with his head buried in his arms on his desk. But near the front of the room, Amy Smith appeared to be wiping a tear out of her eye. Laurie Saunders looked upset too.

'I know many of you are upset,' Ben told the class. 'But I did not show you this film today just to get an emotional reaction from you. I want you to think about what you saw and what I told you. Does anyone have any questions?'

Amy Smith quickly raised her hand.

'Yes, Amy?'

'Were all the Germans Nazis?' she asked.

Ben shook his head. 'No, as a matter of fact, less than ten per cent of the German population belonged to the Nazi Party.'

'Then why didn't anyone try to stop them?' Amy asked.

'I can't tell you for sure, Amy,' Ross told her. 'I can only guess that they were scared. The Nazis might have been a minority, but they were a highly organized, armed, and dangerous minority. You have to remember that the rest of the German population was unorganized, and unarmed and frightened. They had also gone through a terrible period of inflation that had virtually ruined their country. Perhaps some of them hoped the Nazis would be able to restore their society. Anyway, after the war, the majority of Germans said they didn't know about the atrocities.'

Near the front of the room, a young black named Eric raised his hand urgently. 'That's crazy,' he said. 'How could you slaughter ten million people without somebody noticing?'

'Yeah,' said Brad, the boy who had picked on Robert Billings before class began. 'That can't be true.'

It was obvious to Ben that the film had affected a large part of the class, and he was pleased. It was good to see them concerned about something. 'Well,' he said to Eric and Brad, 'I can only tell you that after the war the Germans claimed they knew nothing of the concentration camps or the killings.'

Now Laurie Saunders raised her hand. 'But Eric's right,' she said. 'How could the Germans sit back while the Nazis slaughtered people all around them and say they didn't know about it? How could they do that? How could they even say that?'

'All I can tell you,' Ben said, 'is that the Nazis were highly organized and feared. The behaviour of the rest of the German population is a mystery – why they didn't try to stop it, how they could say they didn't know. We just don't know the answers.'

Eric's hand was up again. 'All I can say is, I would never let such a small minority of people rule the majority.'

'Yeah,' said Brad. 'I wouldn't let a couple of Nazis scare me into pretending I didn't see or hear anything.'

There were other hands raised with questions, but before Ben could call on anyone, the bell rang out and the class was rushing out into the hall.

David Collins stood up. His stomach was grumbling like mad. That morning he'd got up late and had to skip his usual three-course breakfast to make it to school on time. Even though the film Mr Ross had shown really bothered him, he couldn't help thinking that next period was lunch.

He looked over at Laurie Saunders, his girl friend, who was still sitting in her seat. 'Come on, Laurie,' he urged her. 'We have to get down to the cafeteria fast. You know how long the queue gets.'

But Laurie waved him to go without her. 'I'll catch up later.'

David scowled. He was torn between waiting for his girl friend and filling his growling stomach. The stomach won, and David took off down the hall.

After he was gone, Laurie got up from her seat and looked at Mr Ross. There were only a couple of kids left in the room now. And except for Robert Billings, who was just waking up from his nap, they were the ones who seemed the most disturbed about the film. 'I can't even believe that all the Nazis were that cruel,' Laurie told her teacher. 'I don't believe anyone could be that cruel.'

Ben nodded. 'After the war, many Nazis tried to excuse their behaviour by claiming they were only following orders and that they would have been killed themselves if they hadn't.'

Laurie shook her head. 'No, that's no excuse. They could have run away. They could have fought back. They had their own eyes and their own minds. They could think for themselves. Nobody would *just* follow an order like that.'

'But that's what they said,' Ben told her.

Laurie shook her head again. 'It's sick,' she said, her voice filled with revulsion. 'Just totally sick.'

Ben could only nod in agreement.

*

Robert Billings was trying to sneak past Ben's desk.

'Robert,' Ben said. 'Wait a minute.'

The boy froze, but could not look his teacher in the eye.

'Are you getting enough sleep at home?' Ben asked.

Robert nodded dumbly.

Ben sighed. All semester he had been trying to get through to this boy. He couldn't stand seeing him picked on by the other students and it dismayed him that Robert didn't at least try to participate in class. 'Robert,' his teacher said sternly, 'if you don't start participating in this class I will have to fail you. You'll never graduate at this rate.'

Robert glanced at his teacher and then looked away again.

'Don't you have anything to say?' Ben asked.

Robert shrugged. 'I don't care,' he said.

'What do you mean you don't care?' Ben asked.

Robert took a few steps towards the door. Ben could see that he was uncomfortable about being questioned. 'Robert?'

The boy stopped, but he still could not look at his teacher. 'I wouldn't do any good anyway,' he mumbled.

Ben wondered what he could say. Robert's case was a tough one: the younger brother wallowing in the shadow of an older brother who had been the quintessential model student and big man on campus. Jeff Billings had been an all-team pitcher in high school and was now in the Baltimore Orioles minor league while he studied medicine in the off-season. In school he'd been a straight-A student who excelled at everything he did. The kind of guy even Ben had despised in high school.

Seeing that he could never compete with his brother's achievements, Robert had apparently decided it was better not even to try.

'Listen, Robert,' Ben said, 'no one expects you to be another Jeff Billings.'

Robert glanced quickly at Ben and then started chewing nervously on his thumbnail.

'All we're asking is that you try,' Ben said.

'I have to go,' Robert said, looking down at the floor.

'I don't even care about sports, Robert,' Ben said. But the boy had already begun to move slowly towards the door.

Chapter Three

David Collins was sitting in the outdoor courtyard next to the cafeteria. He had already wolfed down half his lunch by the time Laurie arrived, and he was beginning to feel like a normal human being again. He watched Laurie put her tray down next to his and then noticed that Robert Billings was also headed for the court-yard.

'Hey, look,' David whispered as Laurie sat down. They watched as Robert stepped out of the cafeteria carrying a tray, looking for a place to eat. True to form, he had already started eating and stood in the doorway with half a hot dog sticking out of his mouth.

There were two girls from Mr Ross's history class sitting at the table Robert chose. As Robert set his tray down, they both stood up and took their trays to another table. Robert pretended he hadn't noticed.

David shook his head. 'Gordon High's very own Untouchable,' he mumbled.

'Do you think there's something really wrong with him?' Laurie asked.

David shrugged. 'I don't know. He's been pretty strange for as long as I can remember. Then again, if people treated me like that, I'd probably be pretty strange too. It's just weird that he and his brother could come from the same family.'

'Did I ever tell you that my mother knows his mother?' Laurie asked.

'His mother ever talk about him?' David asked.

'No. Except I think she told me once that they had him tested and he really does have a normal I.Q. He's not really dumb or anything.'

'Just weird,' David said and went back to eating his lunch. But Laurie only picked at hers. She seemed preoccupied.

'What is it?' David asked.

'That film, David,' Laurie answered. 'It really bothers me. Doesn't it bother you?'

David thought for a moment. Then he said, 'Yeah, sure, as something horrible that happened once, it bothers me. But that was a long time ago, Laurie. To me it's like a piece of history. You can't change what happened then.'

'But you can't forget it,' Laurie said. She tried a bite of her hamburger, then made a face and put it down.

'Well, you can't go around being bummed out about it for the rest of your life either,' David said. He eyed Laurie's uneaten hamburger. 'By the way, you gonna eat that?'

Laurie shook her head. The movie had left her without much of an appetite. 'Help yourself.'

Not only did David help himself to her burger, he finished off her fries, salad, and ice cream as well. Laurie looked in his direction, but her eyes were distant.

'Hmm.' David wiped his lips with a napkin.

'Would you like anything more?' Laurie asked.

'Well, to tell you the truth . . .'

'Hey, is this seat taken?' someone behind them said.

'I was here first!' said another voice.

David and Laurie looked up to find Amy Smith and Brian Ammon, the quarterback, both heading for their table from opposite directions.

'What do you mean you were here first?' Brian asked.

'Well, I meant I wanted to be here first,' Amy replied.

'Meaning to be first doesn't count,' Brian said. 'Besides, I have to talk to Dave about football.'

'And I have to talk to Laurie,' Amy said.

'What about?' Brian asked.

'Well, about keeping her company while you talk about boring football.'

19

'Stop it,' Laurie said. 'There's room for two.'

'But with them you need room for three,' Amy said, nodding at Brian and David.

'Hardy har har,' Brian grunted.

David and Laurie slid over, and Amy and Brian squeezed in next to them at the table. Amy was right about room for three – Brian was carrying two full lunch trays.

'Hey, what are you doing with all this food?' David asked, patting Brian on the back. Although he was the team's quarterback, Brian was not very big. David stood a full head taller than him.

'I gotta gain some weight,' Brian said as he started to wolf down his lunch. 'I'm gonna need every pound I've got against those guys from Clarkstown on Saturday. They are big. I mean, huge. I hear they got a linebacker who stands six three and weighs sixteen stone.'

'I don't see what you're worried about,' Amy said. 'No one that heavy can run very fast.'

Brian rolled his eyes. 'He doesn't *have* to run, Amy. All he has to do is squash quarterbacks.'

'Will you have a chance on Saturday?' Laurie asked. She was thinking about the story they would need for *The Grapevine*.

David shrugged. 'I don't know. The team's pretty disorganized. We're way behind on learning our plays and stuff. Half the guys don't even show up for practice.'

'Yeah,' Brian agreed. 'Coach Schiller said he was gonna throw anyone who didn't show up for practice off the team. But if he did that we wouldn't even have enough guys to play.'

No one seemed to have anything more to say about football, so Brian bit into his second hamburger.

David's thoughts drifted to other pressing matters. 'Hey, is anyone here good at calculus?'

'Why are you taking calculus?' Amy asked.

'You need it for engineering,' David said.

'So why not wait till college?' Brian asked.

'I heard it was so hard you have to take it twice to understand it,' David explained, 'So I figured I'd take it once now and once later.'

Amy nudged Laurie. 'I think your boyfriend is strange,' she said.

'Talk about strange,' Brian whispered, nodding toward Robert Billings.

They all looked. Robert was sitting alone at his table, engrossed in a Spiderman comic book. His lips moved as he read and there was a red streak of ketchup on his chin.

'You see him sleep through the whole movie?' Brian asked.

'Don't remind Laurie,' David told him. 'She's upset.'

'What, about that movie?' Brian asked.

Laurie gave David a dirty look. 'Do you *have* to tell everybody?'

'Well, it's true, isn't it?' David asked.

'Oh, just leave me alone,' Laurie answered.

'I can understand how you feel,' Amy told her. 'I thought it was just awful.'

Laurie turned to David. 'There, you see? I'm not the only one that it bothered.'

'Hey,' David said defensively. 'I didn't say I wasn't bothered by it. I just said it's over now. Forget about it. It happened once and the world learned its lesson. It'll never happen again.'

'I hope not,' Laurie said, picking up her tray.

'Where're you going?' David asked her.

'I have to go and work on *The Grapevine*,' Laurie said.

'Wait,' Amy said, 'I'll go with you.'

David and Brian watched the two girls go.

'Gee, she really is upset about that movie, isn't she?' Brian said.

'Yeah.' David nodded. 'You know, she always takes stuff like that too seriously.'

Amy Smith and Laurie Saunders sat in *The Grapevine* office talking. Amy wasn't on the newspaper staff, but she often hung out with Laurie in the publications office. The office door could be locked, and Amy would sit inside by an open window, holding a cigarette outside and blowing the smoke out. If a teacher came in, she could drop the cigarette to the ground and there would hardly be any smell of smoke in the room.

'That was an awful movie,' Amy said.

Laurie nodded quietly.

'Are you and David having a fight?' her friend asked.

'Oh, not really.' Laurie couldn't help smiling slightly. 'I just wish he would take something besides football seriously. He's – I don't know – he's such a jock sometimes.'

'But he gets good grades,' Amy said. 'At least he's not a dumb jock like Brian.'

The two girls giggled for a moment and then Amy asked, 'Why does he want to be an engineer? It sounds so boring.'

'He wants to be a computer engineer,' Laurie said. 'Did you ever see the one he has at home? He built it from a kit.'

'Somehow I missed it,' Amy said facetiously. 'By the way, have you decided what you're doing next year?'

Laurie shook her head. 'Maybe we'll go somewhere together. It depends on where we get accepted.'

'Your parents will be thrilled,' Amy said.

'I don't think they'd mind that much,' Laurie said.

'Why don't you just get married?' Amy asked.

Laurie made a face. 'Oh, Amy. I mean, I guess I love David, but who wants to get married yet?'

Amy smiled. 'Oh, I don't know, if David asked *me* I might consider it,' she teased.

Laurie laughed. 'Would you like me to drop a hint?'

'Come off it, Laurie,' Amy said. 'You know how much he likes you. He doesn't even look at other girls.'

'He'd better not,' Laurie said. She noticed that there was a wistful note to Amy's voice. Ever since Laurie had started dating David, Amy had wanted to date a football player too. It sometimes bothered Laurie that underlying their friendship was a constant competition for boys, grades, popularity, almost everything one could compete for. Even though they were best friends, that constant competition somehow prevented them from being really close.

Suddenly there was a loud knock on the door and someone tried the doorknob. Both girls jumped. 'Who is it?' Laurie asked.

'Principal Owens,' a deep voice replied. 'Why is this door locked?'

Amy's eyes went wide with fear. She quickly dropped her cigarette and started digging through her pocket-book for a stick of gum or a mint.

'Uh, it must have been an accident,' Laurie replied nervously, going to the door.

'Well, open it immediately!'

Amy looked terrified.

Laurie gave her a helpless look and pulled the door open.

Outside in the hall were Carl Block, *The Grapevine*'s investigative reporter, and Alex Cooper, the music reviewer. They were both grinning.

'Oh, you two!' Laurie said angrily. Behind her Amy looked as if she was going to faint as the two biggest practical jokers in the school stepped into the room.

Carl was a tall, thin guy with blond hair. Alex, who was stocky and dark, was wearing earphones connected to a small tape player.

'Something illegal going on in here?' Carl asked slyly, making his eyebrows bounce up and down.

'You made me waste a perfectly good cigarette,' Amy complained.

'Tisk, tisk,' Alex said, looking on disapprovingly.

'So how is the paper coming?' Carl asked.

'What do you mean?' Laurie asked in exasperation. 'Neither of you has handed in your assignments for this issue.'

'Oh-oh.' Alex was suddenly looking at his watch and backing away towards the door. 'I just remembered I have to catch a plane to Argentina.'

'I'll drive you to the airport!' Carl said, following him out the door.

Laurie looked at Amy and shook her head wearily. 'Those two,' she mumbled, making a fist.

Chapter Four

Something bothered Ben Ross. He couldn't quite put his finger on it, but he was intrigued by the questions the kids in his history class had asked him after the film that day. It made him wonder. Why hadn't he been able to give the students adequate answers to their questions? Was the behaviour of the majority of Germans during the Nazi regime really so inexplicable?

That afternoon before he left school, Ross had stopped at the library and taken out an armful of books. His wife, Christy, would be playing tennis that evening with some friends, so he knew he would have a long period of uninterrupted time to pursue his thoughts. Now, several hours later, after reading through a number of books, Ben suspected that he would not find the real answer written anywhere. It made him wonder. Was this something historians knew words could not explain? Was it something one could only understand by being there? Or, if possible, by recreating a similar situation?

The idea intrigued Ross. Suppose, he thought, just suppose he took a period, perhaps two periods, and tried an experiment. Just tried to give his students a sampling, a taste of what life in Nazi Germany might have been like. If he could just figure out how it could be done, how the experiment could be run, he was certain it would make far more of an impression on the students than any book explanation could ever make. It certainly was worth a try.

Christy Ross didn't get in that night until after eleven o'clock. She'd played tennis and then had dinner with a friend. She got

24

home to find her husband sitting at their kitchen table surrounded by books.

'Doing your homework?'

'In a way, yes,' Ben Ross replied without looking up from his books.

On top of one of the books Christy noticed an empty glass and an empty plate with a few crumbs from what once must have been a sandwich.

'Well, at least you remembered to feed yourself,' she said, picking up the dish and placing it in the sink.

Her husband didn't answer. His nose was still stuck in the book.

'I bet you're just dying to find out how badly I beat Betty Lewis tonight,' she said, kidding him.

Ben looked up. 'What?'

'I said I beat Betty Lewis tonight,' Christy told him.

Her husband had a blank look on his face.

Christy laughed. 'Betty Lewis. You know, the Betty Lewis who I've never won more than two games in a set from. I beat her tonight. In two sets. Six-four; seven-five.'

'Oh, uh, that's very good,' Ben said absently. He looked back down at the book and started reading again.

Someone else might have been offended by his apparent rudeness, but Christy wasn't. She knew Ben was the kind of person who got involved with things. Not just involved, but utterly absorbed in them to the point where he tended to forget that the rest of the world existed. She'd never forget the time in graduate school when he got interested in American Indians. For months he was so wrapped up in Indians that he forgot about the rest of his life. On weekends he'd visit Indian reservations or spend hours looking for old books in dusty libraries. He even started bringing Indians home for dinner! And wearing deerskin moccasins! Christy used to get up some mornings wondering if he was going to put on war paint.

But that was the way Ben was. One summer she'd taught him to play bridge, and within a month not only was he a better bridge player than she, but he was driving her crazy, insisting that they play bridge every minute of the day. He only calmed down after he won a local bridge tournament and ran out of worthy competitors. It was almost frightening, the way he lost himself in each new adventure.

Christy looked at the books scattered about the kitchen table and sighed. 'What is it this time?' she asked. 'The Indians again? Astronomy? The behavioural characteristics of killer whales?'

When her husband didn't answer, she picked up some of the books. '*The Rise and Fall of the Third Reich? Hitler's Youth?*' She frowned. 'What are you doing, cramming for a degree in dictatorship?'

'Not funny,' Ben muttered without looking up.

'You're right,' Christy admitted.

Ben Ross sat back and looked at his wife. 'One of my students asked me a question today that I couldn't answer.'

'So what else is new?' Christy asked.

'But I don't think I ever saw the answer written anywhere,' Ben told her. 'It just may be an answer they have to learn for themselves.'

Christy Ross nodded. 'Well, I can see what kind of night this is going to be,' she said. 'Just remember, tomorrow you have to be awake enough to teach an entire day of classes.'

Her husband nodded. 'I know, I know.'

Christy Ross bent down and kissed him on his forehead. 'Try not to wake me. *If* you come to sleep tonight.'

Chapter Five

The next day the students drifted in slowly as usual. Some took their seats, others stood around talking. Robert Billings was by the windows, tying knots in the blind cords. While he was doing that, Brad, his incessant tormentor, walked past and patted him on the back, sticking a small sign that said 'kick me' to his shirt.

It looked like just another typical day in history class until the kids noticed that their teacher had written in large letters across the blackboard: STRENGTH THROUGH DIS-CIPLINE.

'What's that supposed to mean?' someone asked.

'I'll tell you just as soon as you're all seated,' Ben Ross answered. When the kids were all in their places, he began to lecture. 'Today I am going to talk to you about discipline.'

A collective groan went up from the seated students. There were some teachers whose classes you knew would be a drag, but most of the students expected Ross's history class to be pretty good – which meant no dumb lectures on stuff like discipline.

'Hold it,' Ben told them. 'Before you make a judgement, give this a chance. It could be exciting.'

'Oh sure,' someone said.

'Oh sure is right,' Ben told his students. 'Now when I talk about discipline, I'm talking about power,' he said, making a fist to accentuate the point. 'And I'm talking about success. Success through discipline. Is there anyone here who isn't interested in power and success?'

'Probably Robert,' Brad said. A bunch of kids snickered.

'Now wait,' Ben told them. 'David, Brian, Eric, you play football. You already know it takes discipline to win.'

'That must be why we haven't won a game in two years,' Eric said, and the class laughed.

It took their teacher a few moments to calm them down again. 'Listen,' he said, gesturing towards a pretty, red-haired student who appeared to be sitting taller in her chair than those around her. 'Andrea, you're a ballet dancer. Doesn't it take ballet dancers long, hard hours of work to develop their skills?'

She nodded, and Ross turned to the rest of the class. 'It's the same with every art. Painting, writing, music – all of them take years of hard work, discipline, and control.'

'So what?' said a student who was slouching down in his chair.

'So what?' Ben asked. 'I'll show you. Suppose I could prove to you that you can create power through discipline. Suppose we could do it right here in this classroom. What would you say to that?'

Ross had expected another wisecrack, and he was surprised when it didn't come. Instead the students were becoming interested and curious. Ben went behind his desk and pulled his wooden chair in front of the room so that all the students could see it.

'All right,' he said. 'Discipline begins with posture. Amy, come up here for a minute.'

As Amy rose, Brian mumbled, 'Teacher's pet.' Normally that would have been enough to start the entire class laughing, but only a few chuckled. The rest ignored him. Everyone was wondering what their teacher was up to.

As Amy sat in the chair at the front of the room, Ben instructed her on how to sit. 'Place your hands flat across the small of your back and force your spine straight up. There, can't you breathe more easily?'

Around the classroom, many of the students were imitating the position they saw Amy taking. But even though they were sitting straighter, some couldn't help finding it humorous. David was the next to try his hand at a joke: 'Is this history, or did I come to phys. ed. by mistake?' he asked. A few kids laughed, but still tried to improve their posture.

'Come on, David,' Ben said. 'Give it a try. We've had enough wise-guy remarks.'

Grudgingly David pushed himself up straight in his chair. Meanwhile their teacher walked down each aisle, checking the posture of each student. It was amazing, Ross thought. Somehow he'd hooked them. Why, even Robert . . .

'Class,' Ben announced, 'I want everyone to see how Robert's legs are parallel. His ankles are locked, his knees are bent at ninety degrees. See how straight his spine is. Chin tucked in, head up. That's very good, Robert.'

Robert, the class nerd, looked up at his teacher and smiled briefly, then returned to his stiff upright position. Around the room the other students tried to copy him.

Ben returned to the front of the classroom. 'All right. Now I want you all to get up and walk around the room. When I give the command, I want you to return to your seats as quickly as possible and assume the proper seating posture. Come on, everyone, up, up, up.'

The students stood up and started wandering around the room. Ben knew he couldn't let them go too long or they'd lose their concentration on the exercise, so he quickly said, 'Take your seats!'

The students dashed back to their seats. There were bumps and grunts as a few ran into each other, and around the room some kids laughed, but the dominant sound was the loud scraping of chair legs as the kids sat down.

In the front of the room, Ben shook his head. 'That was the most disorganized mess I've ever seen. This isn't duck, duck, goose, this is an experiment in movement and posture. Now come on, let's try it again. This time without the chatter. The quicker and more controlled you are, the faster you will be able to reach your seats properly. Okay? Now, everyone, up!'

For the next twenty minutes the class practised getting out of their seats, wandering around in apparent disorganization and then, at their teacher's command, quickly returning to their seats and the correct seated posture. Ben shouted orders more like a drill sergeant than a teacher. Once they seemed to have mastered quick and correct seating, he threw in a new twist. They would still leave their seats and return. But now they would return from the hallway and Ross would time them with a stopwatch.

On the first try, it took forty-eight seconds. The second time they were able to do it in half a minute. Before the last attempt, David had an idea.

'Listen,' he told his classmates as they stood outside in the hall waiting for Mr Ross's signal. 'Let's line up in the order of who has to go the farthest to reach their desks inside. That way we won't have to bump into each other.'

The rest of the class agreed. As they got into the correct order, they couldn't help noticing that Robert was at the head of the line. 'The new head of the class,' someone whispered as they waited nervously for their teacher to give them the sign. Ben snapped his fingers and the column of students moved quickly and quietly into the room. As the last student reached his seat, Ben clicked the stopwatch off. He was smiling. 'Sixteen seconds.'

The class cheered.

'All right, all right, quiet down,' their teacher said, returning to the front of the room. To his surprise, the students calmed down quickly. The silence that suddenly filled the room was almost eerie. Normally the only time the room was that still, Ross thought, was when it was empty.

'Now, there are three more rules that you must obey,' he told them. 'One. Everybody must have pencils and notepaper for note-taking. Two. When asking or answering a question, you must stand at the side of your seats. And three. The first words you say when answering or asking a question are, "Mr Ross." All right?'

Around the room, heads nodded.

'All right,' Mr Ross said. 'Brad, who was the British Prime Minister before Churchill?'

Still sitting at his seat, Brad chewed nervously on a fingernail. 'Uh, wasn't it –'

But before he could say more, Mr Ross quickly cut him off. 'Wrong, Brad, you already forgot the rules I just told you.' He looked across the room at Robert. 'Robert, show Brad the proper procedure for answering a question.'

Instantly Robert stood up next to his desk at attention. 'Mr Ross.'

'Correct,' Mr Ross said. 'Thank you, Robert.'

'Aw, this is dumb,' Brad mumbled.

'Just because you couldn't do it right,' someone said.

'Brad,' Mr Ross said, 'who was the Prime Minister before Churchill?'

This time Brad rose and stood beside his desk. 'Mr Ross, it was, uh, Prime Minister, uh.'

'You're still too slow, Brad,' Mr Ross said. 'From now on, everyone make your answers as short as possible, and spit them out when asked. Now, Brad, try again.'

This time Brad snapped up beside his seat. 'Mr Ross, Chamberlain.'

Ben nodded approvingly. 'Now that's the way to answer a question. Punctual, precise, with punch. Andrea, what country did Hitler invade in September of 1939?'

Andrea, the ballet dancer, stood stiffly by her desk. 'Mr Ross, I don't know.'

Mr Ross smiled. 'Still, a good response because you used proper form. Amy, do you know the answer?'

Amy hopped up beside her desk. 'Mr Ross, Poland.'

'Excellent,' Mr Ross said. 'Brian, what was the name of Hitler's political party?'

Brian quickly got out of his chair. 'Mr Ross, the Nazis.'

Mr Ross nodded. 'That's good, Brian. Very quick. Now, does anyone know the official name of the party? Laurie?'

Laurie Saunders stood up beside her desk. 'The National Socialist –'

'No!' There was a sharp bang as Mr Ross struck his desktop with a ruler. 'Now do it again correctly.'

Laurie sat down, a confused look on her face. What had she done wrong? David leaned over and whispered in her ear. Oh, right. She stood up again. 'Mr Ross, the National Socialist German Workers Party.'

'Correct,' Mr Ross replied.

Mr Ross kept asking questions, and around the room students jumped to attention, eager to show that they knew both the answer and the correct form with which to give it. It was a far cry from the normally casual atmosphere of the classroom, but neither Ben nor his students reflected on that fact. They were too caught up in this new game. The speed and precision of each question and answer were exhilarating. Soon Ben was perspiring as he shouted each question out and another student rose sharply beside his or her desk to shout back a terse reply.

'Peter, who proposed the Lend-Lease Act?'

'Mr Ross, Roosevelt.'

'Right. Eric, who died in the death camps?'

'Mr Ross, the Jews.'

'Anyone else, Brad?'

'Mr Ross, gypsies, homosexuals, and the feebleminded.'

'Good. Amy, why were they murdered?'

'Mr Ross, because they weren't part of the superior race.'

'Correct. David, who ran the death camps?'

'Mr Ross, the S.S.'

'Excellent!'

Out in the hall, the bells were ringing, but no one in the classroom moved from their seat. Still carried by the momentum of the class's progress that period, Ben stood at the front of the room and issued the final order of the day. 'Tonight, finish reading chapter seven and read the first half of chapter eight. That's all, class dismissed.' Before him the class rose in what seemed like a single movement and rushed out into the hall.

'Wow, that was weird, man, it was like a rush,' Brian gasped in uncharacteristic enthusiasm: He and some of the students from Mr Ross's class were standing in a tight pack in the corridor, still riding on the energy they'd felt in the classroom.

'I've never felt anything like that before,' said Eric beside him.

'Well, it sure beats taking notes,' Amy cracked.

'Yeah,' Brian said. He and a couple of other students laughed.

'Hey, but don't knock it,' David said. 'That was really different. It was like, when we all acted together, we were more than just a class. We were a unit. Remember what Mr Ross said about power? I think he was right. Didn't you feel it?'

'Aw, you're taking it too seriously,' said Brad behind him.

'Yeah?' David said. 'Well then, how do you explain it?'

Brad shrugged. 'What's to explain? Ross asked questions, we answered them. It was like any other class except we had to sit up straight and stand next to our desks. I think you're making a big deal out of nothing.'

'I don't know, Brad,' David said as he turned and left the pack of students.

'Where're you going?' Brian asked.

'The john,' David answered. 'Catch up with you in the cafeteria.'

'Okay,' Brian said.

'Hey, remember to sit up straight,' Brad said, and the others laughed.

David pushed through the door to the men's room. He really wasn't sure if Brad was right or not. Maybe he was making a big deal out of nothing, but on the other hand, there had been the feeling, that group unity. Maybe it didn't make that much difference in the classroom. After all, you were just answering questions. But suppose you took that group feeling, that high energy feeling, and got the football team into it. There were some good athletes on the team, it made David mad that they had such a bad record. They really weren't that bad – they were just undermotivated and disorganized. David knew that if he could ever get the team even half as charged up as Mr Ross's history class had been that day, they could tear apart most of the teams in their league.

Inside the men's room David heard the second bell ring, warning students that the next period was about to begin. He stepped out of a stall and was heading to the sinks when he saw someone and stopped abruptly. The men's room had emptied out and only one person was left, Robert. He was standing in front of a mirror, tucking in his shirt, unaware that he wasn't alone. As David watched, the class loser straightened some of the hair on his head and stared at his reflection. Then he snapped to attention and his lips moved silently, as if he was still in Mr Ross's class answering questions.

33

David stood motionless as Robert practised the move again. And again.

Late that night in their bedroom, Christy Ross sat on the side of the bed in her red nightgown and brushed her long auburn hair. Near her Ben was pulling his pyjamas out of a drawer. 'You know,' he said, 'I would have thought they'd all hate it, being ordered around and forced to sit straight and recite answers. Instead they took to it like they'd been waiting for something like this their whole lives. It was weird.'

'Don't you think they were just playing it like a game?' Christy asked. 'Simply competing with each other to see who could be the fastest and straightest?'

'I'm sure that was part of it,' Ben told his wife. 'But even a game is something you either choose to play or not to play. They didn't have to play that game, but they wanted to. The strangest thing was, once we started I could feel them wanting more. They wanted to be disciplined. And each time they mastered one discipline, they wanted another. When the bell rang at the end of the period and they were still in their seats, I knew it meant more to them than just a game.'

Christy stopped brushing her hair. 'You mean they stayed *after* the bell?' she asked.

Ben nodded. 'That's what I mean.'

His wife looked at him sceptically but then grinned. 'Ben, I think you've created a monster.'

'Hardly,' Ben replied, chuckling.

Christy put down her brush and rubbed some cream into her face. On his side of the bed, Ben was pulling on his pyjama top. Christy was waiting for her husband to lean over for their customary goodnight kiss. But tonight it was not forthcoming. He was still lost in thought.

'Ben?' Christy said.

'Yeah?'

'Do you think you'll go on with it tomorrow?'

'I don't think so,' her husband replied. 'We've got to get on to the Japanese campaign.'

Christy closed the jar of cream and settled comfortably into the bed. But on his side Ben still had not moved. He had told his wife how surprisingly enthusiastic his students had been that afternoon, but he had not told her that he too had got caught up in it. It would almost be embarrassing to admit that he could get swept up in such a simple game. But yet on reflection he knew that he had. The fierce exchange of questions and answers, the quest for perfect discipline — it had been infectious and, in a way, mesmerizing. He had enjoyed his students' accomplishment. Interesting, he thought as he got into bed.

Chapter Six

For Ben, what happened the next day was extremely unusual. Instead of his students straggling into class after the bell had rung, it was he who was late. He'd accidentally left his lecture notes and book on Japan in his car that morning and had to run out to the car park before class to get them. As he rushed into the classroom he expected to find a madhouse, but he was in for a surprise.

In his room were five neat rows of desks, seven desks to a row. At each desk a student sat stiffly in the posture Ben had taught them the previous day. The room was silent, and Ross surveyed his class uneasily. Was it a joke? Here and there he saw a face on the verge of smiling, but those were clearly outnumbered by faces at stiff attention, staring straight ahead, concentrating. A few students glanced at him uncertainly – waiting to see if he'd carry it further. Should he? It was such an experience and so different from the norm that it tantalized him. What could they learn from this? What could he learn? Tempted by the unknown, Ben decided it was worth finding out.

'Well, okay,' he said, putting away his notes. 'What's going on here?'

The students looked at him uncertainly.

Ben looked toward the far side of the room. 'Robert?'

Robert Billings quickly rose beside his desk. His shirt was tucked in and his hair was combed. 'Mr Ross, discipline.'

'Yes, discipline,' Mr Ross agreed. 'But that's just part of it. There's something more.' Then he turned to the blackboard, and underneath the large 'STRENGTH THROUGH DIS-CIPLINE' from the day before, he added 'COMMUNITY'.

He turned back to the class. 'Community is the bond between people who work and struggle together for a common goal. It's like building a barn with your neighbours.'

A few students in the room chuckled. But David knew what Mr Ross was saying. It was what he'd thought about yesterday after class. It was the kind of team spirit the football team needed.

'It's the feeling that you're part of something that's more important than yourself,' Mr Ross was telling them. 'You're a movement, a team, a cause. You're committed to something –'

'I think we ought to be committed all right,' someone mumbled, but the near-by students hushed him.

'Like discipline,' Mr Ross continued, 'to understand community fully you have to experience it and participate in it. From now on, our two mottoes will be, "Strength Through Discipline" and "Strength Through Community". Everyone, repeat our mottoes.'

Around the room, students rose beside their desks and recited the slogans: 'Strength Through Discipline, Strength Through Community.'

A few students, including Laurie and Brad, did not join them, but sat uncomfortably in their chairs as Mr Ross had the class repeat the mottoes again. Finally Laurie rose, and then Brad. Now the entire class stood beside their desks.

'What we need now is a symbol for our new community,' Mr Ross told them. He turned back to the board and, after a moment's thought, drew a circle with the outline of a wave inside it. 'This will be our symbol. A wave is a pattern of change. It has movement, direction, and impact. From now on, our community, our movement will be known as The Wave.' He paused and looked at the class standing at stiff attention, accepting everything he told them. 'And this will be our salute,' he said, cupping his right hand in the shape of a wave, then tapping it against his left shoulder and holding it upright. 'Class, give the salute,' he ordered.

The class gave the salute. Some hit their right shoulders instead of their left. Others forgot to hit their shoulders entirely. 'Again,'

Ross ordered, making the salute himself. He repeated the exercise until everyone had it right.

'All right,' their teacher said when they'd got it. Once again the class could feel the resurgence of power and unity that had overwhelmed them the day before. 'This is our salute and our salute only,' he told them. 'Whenever you see another Wave member, you will salute. Robert, salute and give our mottoes.'

Standing stiffly beside his seat, Robert performed the salute and replied, 'Mr Ross, Strength Through Discipline, Strength Through Community.'

'Very good,' Ben said. 'Peter, Amy, and Eric, salute and recite our motto with Robert.'

The four students obediently saluted and chanted, 'Strength Through Discipline, Strength Through Community.'

'Brian, Andrea, and Laurie,' Mr Ross commanded. 'Join them and repeat.'

Now seven students joined in the chant, then fourteen, then twenty, until the whole class was saluting and chanting loudly in unison. 'Strength Through Discipline, Strength Through Community.' Like a regiment, Ben thought, just like a regiment.

In the gym after school, David, and Eric sat on the floor in their football practice jerseys. They were a little early for practice and were having a heated debate.

'I think it's dumb,' Eric said as he tied the laces on his cleats. 'It's just a game in history class, that's all.'

'But that doesn't mean it couldn't work,' David insisted. 'What do you think we learned it for, anyway? To keep it a secret? I'm telling you, Eric, this is just what the team needs.'

'Well, you're gonna have to convince Coach Schiller of that,' Eric said. 'And I'm not going to tell him.'

'What are you scared of?' David asked. 'You think Mr Ross is gonna punish me because I tell a couple of people about The Wave?'

Eric shrugged. 'No, man. I think they're gonna laugh.'

Brian came out of the locker room and joined them on the floor.

'Hey,' David said, 'what do you think of us trying to get the rest of the team into The Wave?'

Brian tugged at his shoulder pads and thought about it. 'You think The Wave could stop that sixteen stone linebacker from Clarkstown?' he asked. 'I swear, that's all I think about. I keep picturing me calling for the ball and then this thing appears in front of me, this giant thing in a Clarkstown uniform. It steps on my centre, it squashes my guards. It's so big I can't go left, I can't go right, I can't throw over it . . .' Brian rolled on his back on the floor and pretended someone was bearing down on him. 'It just keeps coming and coming. Ahhhhhhhhhh!'

Eric and David laughed, and Brian sat up. 'I'll do anything,' he told them. 'Eat my Wheaties, join The Wave, do my homework. Anything to stop that guy.'

More players had gathered around them, including a junior named Deutsch, who was the second-string quarterback behind Brian. Everyone on the team knew that Deutsch wanted nothing more in the world than to steal Brian's position from him. As a result, the two of them didn't get along.

'I hear you say you're afraid of the Clarkstown team?' Deutsch asked Brian. 'I'll take your place, man, just say the word.'

'They let you into the game and we'll have no chance at all,' Brian told him.

Deutsch sneered. 'The only reasons you're first string is 'cause you're a senior,' he said.

Still sitting on the gym floor, Brian gazed up at the junior. 'Man, you are the most conceited bag of no talent I've ever seen,' he said.

'Oh yeah, look who's talking,' Deutsch snarled back.

The next thing David knew, Brian had jumped to his feet and had his fists up. David lunged between the two quarterbacks.

'That's just what I was talking about!' he yelled as he pushed them apart. 'We're supposed to be a team. We're supposed to support each other. The reason we've been so bad is because all we've been doing is fighting with each other.'

More football players were in the gym now. 'What's he talking about?' one of them asked.

David turned. 'I'm talking about unity. I'm talking about discipline. We have to start acting like a team. Like we have a common

39

goal. Your job on this team isn't to steal another guy's position. Your job is to help this team win.'

'I could help this team win,' Deutsch said. 'All Coach Schiller's got to do is make me the first-string quarterback.'

'No, man!' David yelled at him. 'A bunch of self-serving individuals don't make a team. You know why we've done so bad this year? Because we're twenty-five one-man teams all wearing the same Gordon High uniforms. You want to be first-string quarterback on a team that doesn't win? Or do you want to be second-string on a team that does win?'

Deutsch shrugged.

'I'm tired of losing,' said another player.

'Yeah,' said someone else. 'It's a drag. This school doesn't even take us seriously any more.'

'I'd give up my position and be a waterboy if it meant winning a game,' said a third.

'Well, we could win,' said David. 'I'm not saying we'll be able to go out and destroy Clarkstown on Saturday, but if we start trying to be a team, I bet we could win a few games this year.'

Most of the members of the football team were there by this time, and as David looked around at their faces he could see that they were interested.

'Okay,' said one. 'What do we do?'

David hesitated for a moment. What they could do was The Wave. But who was he to tell them? He'd only learned of it the day before himself. Suddenly he felt someone nudging him.

'Tell them,' Eric whispered. 'Tell 'em about The Wave.'

What the hell, David thought. 'Okay, all I know is you gotta start by learning the mottoes. And this is the salute . . .'

Chapter Seven

That evening Laurie Saunders told her parents about her last two days of history class. The Saunders family was sitting at the dining-room table finishing dinner. Through most of the meal, Laurie's father had given them a stroke-by-stroke description of the 78 he'd shot in golf that afternoon. Mr Saunders ran a division of a large semiconductor company. Laurie's mother said that she didn't mind his passion for golf because on the course he managed to get out all the pressures and frustrations of his job. She said she couldn't explain how he did it, but as long as he came home in a good mood, she wasn't going to argue.

Neither was Laurie, although listening to her father talk about his golf game sometimes bored her to death. It was better that he was easy-going, rather than a worry-wart like her mother, who was probably the brightest and most perceptive woman Laurie had ever encountered. She practically ran the county's League of Women Voters by herself and was so politically astute that aspiring politicians seeking local offices were always asking her to advise them.

For Laurie, her mother was lots of fun when things were going well. She was full of ideas, and you could talk to her for hours. But other times, when Laurie was upset about something or was having a problem, her mother was murder – there was no way to hide anything from her. And once Laurie had admitted what the difficulty was, she wouldn't leave her alone.

When Laurie had started telling them about The Wave at dinner, it was mostly because she couldn't stand listening to her father talk about golf for another minute. She could tell her mother was

41

bored too. For the last quarter of an hour Mrs Saunders had been scratching a wax stain out of the tablecloth with her fingernail.

'It was incredible,' Laurie was saying about the class. 'Everyone was saluting and repeating the motto. You couldn't help but get caught up in it. You know, really wanting to make it work. Feeling all that energy building around you.'

Mrs Saunders stopped scratching the tablecloth and looked at her daughter. 'I don't think I like it, Laurie. It sounds too militaristic to me.'

'Oh, Mom,' Laurie said, 'you always take things the wrong way. It's nothing like that. Honest, you'd just have to be there feeling the positive energy in the class to really get what's going on.'

Mr Saunders agreed. 'To tell you the truth, I'm for whatever will make these kids pay attention to anything these days.'

'And that's what it's really doing, Mom,' Laurie said. 'Even the bad kids are into it. You know Robert Billings, the class creep? Even he's part of a group. No one's picked on him for two whole days. Tell me that isn't positive.'

'But you're supposed to be learning history,' Mrs Saunders argued. 'Not how to be part of a group.'

'Well, you know,' her husband said, 'this country was built by people who were part of a group – the Pilgrims, the Founding Fathers. I don't think it's wrong for Laurie to be learning how to co-operate. If I could get some more co-operation down at the plant instead of this constant back-biting and bickering and everyone trying to cover his own you-know-what, we wouldn't be behind in production this year.'

'I didn't say that it was wrong to co-operate,' Mrs Saunders replied. 'But still, people have to do things in their own way. You talk about the greatness of this country and you're talking about people who weren't afraid to act as individuals.'

'Mom, I really think you're taking this the wrong way,' Laurie said. 'Mr Ross has just found a way to get everybody involved. And we're still doing our homework. It's not like we've forgotten about history.'

But her mother was not to be appeased. 'That's all very well and good. But it just doesn't sound like the right thing for you, Laurie. Babe, we've raised you to be an individual.'

Laurie's father turned to his wife. 'Midge, don't you think you're taking all this a little too seriously? A little bit of community spirit is a terrific thing for these kids.'

'That's right, Mom,' Laurie said, smiling. 'Haven't you always said that I was a little too independent?'

Mrs Saunders was not amused. 'Honey, just remember that the popular thing is not always the right thing.'

'Oh, Mom,' Laurie said, annoyed that her mother would not see her side of the argument at all. 'Either you're being stubborn or you just don't understand this at all.'

'Really, Midge,' Mr Saunders said. 'I'm sure Laurie's history teacher knows exactly what he's doing. I don't see why you should make this into a big deal.'

'You don't think it's dangerous to allow a teacher to manipulate students like that?' Mrs Saunders asked her husband.

'Mr Ross isn't manipulating us,' Laurie said. 'He's one of my best teachers. He knows what he's doing and, as far as I'm concerned, what he's doing is for the class's good. I wish some of my other teachers were as interesting.'

Laurie's mother seemed ready to keep arguing, but her husband changed the subject. 'Where's David tonight?' he asked. 'Isn't he coming over?' David often came over in the evening, usually on the pretence of studying with Laurie. But inevitably he'd wind up in the den with Mr Saunders talking about sports or engineering. Since David hoped to study engineering just as Mr Saunders had, they had lots to talk about. Mr Saunders had also played high school football. Mrs Saunders had once told Laurie that it was surely a match made in heaven.

Laurie shook her head. 'He's home studying tomorrow's history assignment.'

Mr Saunders looked surprised. 'David studying? Now *there's* something to be concerned about.'

Because Ben and Christy Ross both taught full time at the high school, they had grown accustomed to sharing many of the after-school chores around their house – cooking, cleaning, and running errands. That afternoon Christy had to take her car to the garage to get the exhaust replaced, so Ben had agreed that he'd cook. But after that history class he felt too preoccupied to bother cooking. Instead he stopped at the Chinese take away place on the way home and picked up some egg-rolls and egg foo yung.

When Christy got home around dinnertime, she found the table not covered with plates for dinner, but with books, again. Looking over the brown paper take-away bags on the kitchen counter, she asked, 'You call this dinner?'

Ben looked up from the table. 'I'm sorry, Chris. I'm just so preoccupied with this class. And I've got so much to do to prepare for it, I didn't want to take time to cook.'

Christy nodded. It wasn't as if he did this every time it was his turn to cook. She could forgive him this time. She started unpacking the food. 'So how is your experiment going, Dr Frankenstein? Have your monsters turned on you yet?'

'On the contrary,' her husband replied. 'Most of them are actually turning into human beings!'

'You don't say,' said Christy.

'I happen to know that they're all keeping up on their reading,' Ben said. 'Some of them are even reading ahead. It's as if they suddenly love being prepared for class.'

'Or they're suddenly afraid of being unprepared,' his wife observed.

But Ben ignored her comment. 'No, I really think they've improved. At least, they're behaving better.'

Christy shook her head. 'These can't be the same kids I have for music.'

'I'm telling you,' her husband said, 'it's amazing how much more they like you when you make decisions for them.'

'Sure, it means less work for *them*. They don't have to think for themselves,' Christy said. 'But now stop reading and clear some of those books away so we can eat.'

As Ben made room on the kitchen table, Christy set the food out. When Ben stood up Christy thought he was going to help her, but instead he started pacing around the kitchen, deep in thought.

Christy went on getting the meal ready, but she too was thinking about The Wave. There was something about it that bothered her, something about the tone of her husband's voice when he spoke about his class — as if they were now better students than the rest of the school. As she sat down at the table she said, 'How far do you plan to push this, Ben?'

'I don't know,' Ross answered. 'But I think it could be fascinating to see.'

Christy watched her husband pace around the kitchen, lost in thought. 'Why don't you sit down?' she said. 'Your egg foo yung's going to get cold.'

'You know,' her husband said as he came to the table and sat down, 'the funny thing is, I feel myself getting caught up in it too. It's contagious.'

Christy nodded. That was obvious. 'Maybe you're becoming a guinea pig in your own experiment,' she said. Although she made it sound like a joke, she was hoping he'd take it as a warning.

Chapter Eight

Both David and Laurie lived within walking distance of Gordon High. David's route didn't necessarily lead past Laurie's house, but ever since tenth grade he'd always gone out of his way. When he first noticed her, as a sophomore, he used to walk down her street on the way to school every morning, hoping that he would pass her house just as she was leaving for school. At first he managed to run into her only about once a week. But as the weeks passed and they got to know each other, he began to catch her more frequently until, by the spring, they walked together almost every day. For a long time David thought this was just a matter of luck and good timing. It never occurred to him that from the beginning Laurie had waited at her window, watching for him. At first she had only pretended to 'run into' him once a week. Later she 'ran into' him more often.

When David picked Laurie up to walk with her to school the next morning, he was bursting with brainstorms. 'I'm telling you, Laurie,' he said as they walked along a pavement towards school. 'This is just what the football team needs.'

'What the football team needs,' Laurie told him, 'is a quarterback who can pass, a running back who doesn't fumble, a couple of linebackers who aren't afraid to tackle, an end who –'

'Stop it,' David said irritably. 'I'm serious. I got the team into it yesterday. Brian and Eric helped me. The guys really responded to it. I mean, it's not like we improved in only one practice, but I

46

could feel it. I could really feel the team spirit. Even Coach Schiller was impressed. He said we were like a new team.'

'My mother says it sounds like brainwashing to her,' Laurie said.

'What?'

'She says Mr Ross is manipulating us.'

'She's crazy,' David said. 'How could she know? And besides, what do you care what your mother says? You know she worries about everything.'

'I didn't say I agreed with her,' Laurie said.

'Well, you didn't say you disagreed with her either,' David said.

'I was just telling you what she said,' Laurie replied.

David wouldn't let it drop. 'How does she know, anyway? She can't possibly understand what The Wave is about unless she's been in class to see it work. Parents always think they know everything!'

Laurie suddenly felt an urge to disagree with him, but she restrained herself. She didn't want to start a fight with David over something so petty. She hated it when they quarrelled. Besides, for all she knew, The Wave might be just what the football team needed. They certainly needed *something*. She decided to change the subject. 'Did you find help for calculus?'

David shrugged. 'Naw, the only kids who know anything are in my class.'

'So why not ask one of them?'

'No way,' David said. 'I don't want any of them to know I'm having trouble.'

'Why not?' Laurie asked. 'I'm sure someone would help you.'

'Of course they would,' David said. 'But I don't want their help.'

Laurie sighed. It was true that lots of kids at school were competitive about grades and class standing. But few took it as far as David did. 'Well,' she said, 'I know Amy didn't say anything at lunch, but if you can't find anyone else she could probably help you.'

'Amy?'

'She's incredibly smart in maths,' Laurie explained. 'I bet you

47

could give her your problem and she'd have it figured out in ten minutes.'

'But I asked her at lunch,' David said.

'She was just being shy,' Laurie said. 'I think she likes Brian and she just doesn't want to intimidate him by seeming too brainy.'

David laughed. 'I don't think she has to worry, Laurie. The only way she could intimidate him was if she weighed sixteen stone and wore a Clarkstown uniform.'

When the students arrived in class that day, there was a large poster in the back of the room with a blue wave symbol on it. They found Mr Ross dressed differently than usual. Where before he'd come to class in casual clothes, today he wore a blue suit, white shirt, and a tie. The students went quickly to their seats as their teacher walked up and down the aisles passing out small yellow cards.

Brad nudged Laurie. 'It's not time for report cards,' he whispered.

Laurie stared at the card she'd received. 'It's a Wave membership card,' she whispered back.

'What?' Brad hissed.

'All right,' Mr Ross slapped his hands together loudly. 'No talking.'

Brad sat up straight in his seat. But Laurie understood his surprise. Membership cards? It must have been a joke. Meanwhile, Mr Ross had finished distributing the cards and stood in the front of the room.

'Now you will all have membership cards,' Mr Ross announced. 'If you turn them over you will find that some of them have been marked with a red X. If you have a red X you are to be a monitor, and you will report directly to me any members of The Wave who do not obey our rules.'

Around the room students were scrutinizing their cards and turning them over to see if they had a red X. Those who had them, like Robert and Brian, were smiling. Those who didn't, like Laurie, seemed less pleased.

Laurie raised her hand.

'Yes, Laurie,' Ben said.

'Uh, what's the point of this?' Laurie asked.

There was a silence around the room and Ben did not answer right away. Then he said, 'Aren't you forgetting something?'

'Oh, right.' Laurie got up and stood next to her desk. 'Mr Ross, what's the point of these cards?'

Ben had expected someone to question him on the cards. The reason for them would not be apparent immediately. For now he said, 'It's just an example of how a group might monitor itself.'

Laurie had no other questions, so Ben turned to the blackboard and added another word to 'Strength Through Discipline, Strength Through Community'. Today's word was 'Action'.

'Now that we understand Discipline and Community,' he told the class, 'Action is our next lesson. Ultimately, discipline and community are meaningless without action. Discipline gives you the right to action. A disciplined group with a goal can take action to achieve it. They *must* take action to achieve it. Class, do you believe in The Wave?'

There was a split-second hesitation, and then the class rose in unison and answered in what seemed like a single voice. 'Mr Ross, yes!'

Mr Ross nodded. 'Then you must take action! Never be afraid to act on what you believe. As The Wave you must act together like a well-oiled machine. Through hard work and allegiance to each other, you will learn faster and accomplish more. But only if you support one another, and only if you work together and obey the rules, can you ensure the success of The Wave.'

As he spoke, the class members stood beside their desks at attention. Laurie Saunders stood with them, but she did not feel the high energy and unity she'd felt on previous days. In fact, today there was something about the class, something about their single-mindedness and absolute obedience to Mr Ross that she would almost describe as creepy.

'Be seated,' Mr Ross ordered, and instantly the class sat. Their teacher continued his lesson. 'When we first began The Wave a few days ago I felt that some of you were actually competing to give the right answers and to be better members than others. From now on I want this to end. You are not competing against each other, you are working together for a common cause. You must conceive of yourselves as a team, a team of which you are all members. Remember, in The Wave you are all equals. No one is more important or more popular than anyone else and no one is to be excluded from the group. Community means equality within the group.

'Now your first action as a team will be to actively recruit new members. To become a member of The Wave, each new student must demonstrate knowledge of our rules and pledge strict obedience to them.'

David smiled as Eric looked over at him and winked. This was what he'd needed to hear. There was nothing wrong with turning other kids on to The Wave. It was for the good of everybody. Especially the football team.

Mr Ross had concluded his talk on The Wave. He intended to spend the rest of the period reviewing the assignment he'd given the class the night before. But suddenly a student named George Snyder was raising his hand.

'Yes, George.'

George sprang from his seat to attention by his desk. 'Mr Ross, for the first time I feel like I'm part of something,' he announced. 'Something great.'

Around the room, startled students stared at George. Feeling the eyes of the class upon him, George began to sink back into his chair. But then Robert suddenly stood.

'Mr Ross,' he said proudly, 'I know just how George feels. It's like being born again.'

No sooner had he returned to his seat than Amy stood. 'George's right, Mr Ross. I feel the same way.'

David was pleased. He knew that what George had done was corny, but then Robert and Amy had done it too, just so George wouldn't feel foolish and alone. That's what was good about The Wave. They supported each other. Now he stood up and said, 'Mr Ross, I'm proud of The Wave.'

This sudden outburst of testimonials surprised Ben. He was

determined to get on to the day's classwork, but suddenly he knew he had to go along with the class a little longer. Almost subconsciously he sensed how much they wanted him to lead them, and it was something he felt he could not deny.

'Our salute!' he ordered. Around the room students jumped to attention beside their desks and gave The Wave salute. The mottoes followed: 'Strength Through Discipline, Strength Through Community, Strength Through Action!'

Mr Ross was picking up his class notes when the students burst forth again, this time giving the salute and chanting their motto without prompting. Then silence fell over the room. Mr Ross gazed at the students in wonderment. The Wave was no longer just an idea or a game. It was a living movement in his students. They *were* The Wave now, and Ben realized that they could act on their own without him if they wanted. That thought could have been frightening, but Ben was confident that he had control as their leader. The experiment was simply becoming much more interesting.

At lunch that day all The Wave members who were in the cafeteria sat at a single long table. Brian, Brad, Amy, Laurie, and David were there. At first Robert Billings seemed tentative about joining them, but when David saw him he insisted he sit at the table, telling him they were all part of The Wave now.

Most of the kids were raving about what was going on in Mr Ross's class, and Laurie really had no reason to argue with them. But still she felt odd – all that saluting and chanting. Finally, during a pause in the conversation, she said, 'Does anyone feel kind of strange about this?'

David turned to her. 'What do you mean?'

'I don't know,' Laurie said. 'But doesn't it feel a little weird?'

'It's just so different,' Amy told her. 'That's why it feels weird.'

'Yeah,' Brad said. 'It's like there's no in-crowd any more. Man, the thing that bugs me the most about school sometimes is all these little cliques. I'm tired of feeling like every day's a big popularity contest. That's what's so great about The Wave. You don't have to worry about how popular you are. We're all equal. We're all part of the same community.'

'Do you think everyone likes that?' Laurie asked.

'Do you know anyone who doesn't?' David asked.

Laurie felt her face grow flushed. 'Well, I'm not sure I do.'

Suddenly Brian pulled something out of his pocket and held it up to Laurie. 'Hey, don't forget,' he said. He was holding up his Wave membership card with the red X on the back.

'Forget what?' Laurie asked.

'You know,' Brian said. 'What Mr Ross said about reporting anyone who breaks the rules.'

Laurie was shocked. Brian really couldn't be serious, could he? Now Brian started to grin, and she relaxed.

'Besides,' David said. 'Laurie isn't breaking any rule.'

'If she was really against The Wave she would be,' Robert said.

The rest of the table became silent, surprised that Robert had said anything. Some of them weren't even used to hearing his voice, he usually said so little.

'What I mean is,' Robert said nervously, 'the whole idea of The Wave is that the people in it have to support it. If we're really a community, we all have to agree.'

Laurie was about to say something, but she stopped herself. It was The Wave that had given Robert the courage to sit at the table with them and to join in the conversation. If she argued against The Wave now, she would really be implying that Robert should go and sit by himself again and not be part of their 'community'.

Brad patted Robert on his back. 'Hey, I'm glad you joined us,' he said.

Robert blushed and then turned to David. 'Did he stick anything on my back?' he asked. Everyone at the table laughed.

Chapter Nine

Ben Ross wasn't quite sure what to make of The Wave. What had begun as a simple history experiment had become a fad that was spreading outside his classroom. As a result, some unexpected things had started to occur. For one, the size of his daily history class was beginning to expand as students from free periods, study halls, and lunch came to be part of The Wave. The recruiting of more students for The Wave had apparently been far more successful than he had ever expected. So successful, in fact, that Ben began to suspect that some students were cutting other classes to sit in on his.

Remarkably enough, though, even with the larger class size and the students' insistence on practising the salute and motto, the class was not falling behind. If anything, they were covering their assigned lessons even faster than usual. Using the rapid question and answer style that The Wave had inspired, they had quickly covered Japan's entrance into World War Two. Ben noticed a marked improvement in preparation for class and in class participation, but he also noticed that there was less thinking behind the preparation. His students could glibly spit back answers as if by rote, but there was no analysis, no questioning on their part. In a way he could not fault them, because he himself had introduced them to the ways of The Wave. It was just another unexpected development in the experiment.

Ben reasoned that the students realized that to neglect their studies would be detrimental to The Wave. The only way they could have time to spend on The Wave was to be so well prepared that they only needed half the regular class to cover their assigned lessons. But he wasn't certain this was something to be pleased about. The class's homework assignments had improved, but rather than long, thoughtful answers, they wrote short ones. On a multiple choice test they might all do well, but Ben had his doubts about how they'd do on an exam consisting of essays.

To add to the interesting developments in his experiment was a report he'd heard that David Collins and his friends Eric and Brian had successfully infused The Wave into the school's football team. Over the years, Norm Schiller, the biology teacher who also coached the school's football team, had become so soured by wise-cracks about the team's continual losses that during football season he practically went months without speaking to another teacher. But that morning in the faculty lounge Norm had actually thanked him for introducing The Wave to his students. Would wonders never cease?

On his own, Ben had tried to find out what it was that attracted students to The Wave. Some of those he asked said it was just something new and different, like any fad. Others said they liked the democracy of it – the fact that they were all equals now. It pleased Ross to hear that answer. He enjoyed thinking that he had helped break down the petty popularity contests and cliques that he felt often preoccupied too much of his students' thinking and energy. A few students even said they thought the idea of increased discipline was good for them. They had surprised Ben. Over the years, discipline had become an increasingly personal re-sponsibility. If the students didn't do it themselves, their teachers were less and less inclined to step in. Maybe this was a mistake, Ben thought. Perhaps one of the results of his experiment would be a general rebirth of school discipline. He even daydreamed about a story in the education section of *Time* magazine: *Discipline Returns to the Classroom: Teacher Makes Startling Discovery*.

Laurie Saunders sat on a desk in the school publications office, chewing on the end of a pen. Various members of *The Gordon Grapevine* staff sat on desks around her, biting their nails or chew-ing gum. Alex Cooper was wearing his Sony radio and was bopping to the music through his earphones. Another reporter was wearing roller skates. This was *The Grapevine*'s excuse for a weekly editorial meeting.

'Okay,' Laurie told them. 'We've got the same problem as usual. The paper is due out next week, but we don't have enough stories.' Laurie looked at the girl wearing roller skates. 'Jeanie, you were supposed to do a fashion story on the latest clothes. Where is it?'

'Oh, nobody's wearing anything interesting this year,' Jeanie replied. 'It's always the same thing: jeans and sneakers and T-shirts.'

'Well then write about how there are no new styles this year,' Laurie said, then she turned to the reporter who was bopping to his radio. 'Alex?'

Alex kept bopping. He couldn't hear her.

'Alex!' Laurie said more loudly.

Finally someone near Alex gave him a nudge. He looked up, startled. 'Uh, yeah?'

Laurie rolled her eyes. 'Alex, this is supposed to be an editorial meeting.'

'Really?' Alex replied.

'Okay, so where's your record review for this issue?' Laurie asked.

'Oh, uh, yeah, record review, right, uh yeah,' Alex said. 'Well, uh, you see, it's a long story. Uh, like I was going to do it but, uh, remember that trip I said I had to take to Argentina?'

Laurie rolled her eyes again.

'Well, it fell through,' Alex said. 'And I had to go to Hong Kong instead.'

Laurie turned to Alex's sidekick, Carl. 'I suppose you had to go to Hong Kong with him,' she said sarcastically.

Carl shook his head. 'No,' he replied seriously, 'I made the trip to Argentina as scheduled.'

'I see,' said Laurie. She looked around at the rest of *The Grapevine*'s staff. 'I suppose the rest of you have been too busy hopping around the globe to get anything written as well.'

'I went to the movies,' Jeanie said.

'Did you write a review?' Laurie asked.

'No, it was too good,' she replied.

'Too good?'

'It's no fun writing reviews of good movies,' she said.

'Yeah,' said Alex, the globe-hopping record reviewer. 'It's no fun doing a review of a good movie because you can't say anything bad about it. The only time it's fun to review something is when it's bad. Then you can tear it to shreds, he, he, he.' Alex started rubbing his hands together as he went into his mad scientist routine. Alex had the best mad scientist routine in school. He also did a great imitation of a wind surfer in a hurricane.

'We need stories for the paper,' Laurie said resolutely. 'Doesn't anyone have any ideas?'

'They got a new school bus,' someone said.

'Whoopee!'

'I heard that Mr Gabondi's going on sabbatical next year.'

'Maybe he won't come back.'

'Some kid in the tenth grade put his fist through a window yesterday. He was trying to prove that you could punch a hole in a window and not cut yourself.'

'Did he do it?'

'Nope, got twelve stitches.'

'Hey, wait a minute,' said Carl. 'What about this Wave thing? Everyone wants to know what it is.'

'Aren't you in Ross's history class, Laurie?' another staff member asked.

'That's probably the biggest story in school right now,' said a third.

Laurie nodded. She was aware that The Wave was worth a story, and maybe a big story at that. A couple of days ago it had even occurred to her that something like The Wave was probably just what the sluggish, disorganized staff of *The Grapevine* itself needed. But she had set the idea aside. She couldn't even explain her decision consciously. It was just that creepy feeling she'd begun to get, the feeling that maybe they should be careful with The Wave. So far she'd seen it do some good in Mr Ross's class and David said he thought it was helping the football team. But still she was cautious.

'Well, what about it, Laurie?' someone asked.

'The Wave?' Laurie said.

'How come you haven't assigned that story to us?' Alex asked. 'Or are you just saving the good ones for yourself?'

'I don't know if anyone knows enough about it to write about it yet,' Laurie said.

'What do you mean? You're in The Wave, aren't you?' Alex asked.

'Well, yes I am,' Laurie replied. 'But I still ... I still don't know.'

A couple of the staff members scowled. 'Well, I think *The Grapevine* still should have a story reporting that it exists, at least,' Carl said. 'I mean, a lot of kids are wondering what it is.'

Laurie nodded. 'Okay, you're right. I'll try to explain what it is. But in the meantime, I want you all to do something. Since we still have a few days before the paper has to come out. Try to find out everything you can about what kids think of The Wave.'

Ever since the night she had first discussed The Wave with her mother and father at dinner, Laurie had purposely avoided the subject at home. It didn't seem worth creating any more hassles, especially with her mother, who could find something to worry about in everything Laurie did, whether it was going out late with David, chewing on a pen, or The Wave. Laurie just hoped her mother would forget about it. But that night while she was studying in her room her mother knocked on the door. 'Babe, can I come in?'

'Sure, Mom.'

The door opened and Mrs Saunders stepped in, wearing a yellow terrycloth bathrobe and slippers. The skin around her eyes looked greasy, and Laurie knew she'd been putting wrinkle cream on.

'How're the crow's feet, Mom?' she asked in goodnatured humour.

Mrs Saunders smiled wryly at her daughter. 'Some day,' she said, wagging a finger, 'some day you won't think it's so funny.' She walked over to the desk and peered over her daughter's shoulders at the book she was reading. 'Shakespeare?'

'What'd you expect?' Laurie asked.

'Well, anything except The Wave,' Mrs Saunders said, sitting down on her daughter's bed.

Laurie turned to look at her. 'What do you mean, Mom?'

'Only that I met Elaine Billings at the supermarket today, and she told me Robert is a completely new person.'

'Was she worried?' Laurie asked.

'No, she wasn't, but I am,' Mrs Saunders said. 'You know, they've been having problems with him for years. Elaine has talked to me frequently about it. She's been very worried.'

Laurie nodded.

'So she's ecstatic about this sudden change,' Mrs Saunders said. 'But somehow I don't trust it. Such a dramatic personality change. It almost sounds like he's joined a cult or something.'

'What do you mean?'

'Laurie, if you study the types of people who join these cults, they're almost always people who are unhappy with themselves and their lives. They look at the cult as a way of changing, of starting over, of literally being born again. How else do you explain the change in Robert?'

'But what's wrong with that, Mom?'

'The problem is that it's not real, Laurie. Robert is safe only as long as he keeps within the confines of The Wave. But what do you think happens when he leaves it? The outside world doesn't know or care about The Wave. If Robert couldn't function in school before The Wave, he won't be able to function outside school where The Wave doesn't exist.'

Laurie understood. 'Well, you don't have to worry about me, Mom. I don't think I'm as crazy about it as I was a couple of days ago.'

Mrs Saunders nodded. 'No, I didn't think you would be, once you thought about it for a while.'

'So what's the problem?' Laurie asked.

'The problem is everyone else at school who still takes it seriously,' her mother said.

'Oh, Mom, you're the one who's taking this too seriously. Do you want to know what I think? I think it's just a fad. It's like punk rock or something. In two months no one will even remember what The Wave was.'

'Mrs Billings told me that they're organizing a Wave rally for Friday afternoon,' Mrs Saunders said.

'It's just a pep rally for the football game on Saturday,' Laurie explained. 'The only difference is they're calling it a Wave rally instead of a pep rally.'

'At which they will formally indoctrinate two hundred new members?' Mrs Saunders asked sceptically.

Laurie sighed. 'Mom, listen to me. You're really getting paranoid about this whole thing. Nobody's indoctrinating anyone. They're going to welcome new members to The Wave at the rally. Those people would have come to the pep rally anyway. Really, Mom, The Wave is just a game. It's like little boys playing soldier. I wish you could meet Mr Ross because then you'd see there's nothing to worry about. He's such a good teacher. He'd never get into anything like cults.'

'And you're not disturbed by it at all?' Mrs Saunders asked.

'Mom, the only thing that disturbs me is that so many kids in my class could allow themselves to get caught up in something so immature. I mean, I guess I can understand why David is into it. He's convinced that it's going to turn the football team into a winner. But it's Amy I can't understand. I mean, well, you know Amy. She's so bright and yet, I see her taking this so seriously.'

'So you *are* worried,' her mother said.

But Laurie shook her head. 'No, Mom. That's the only thing that bothers me, and that isn't much. I promise you, Mom, this is a molehill and you're looking for a mountain. Really, trust me.'

Mrs Saunders rose slowly. 'Well, all right, Laurie. At least I know you're not involved in this situation. I suppose that's enough to be thankful for. But please, babe, be careful.' She leaned over, kissed her daughter on the forehead, and left the room.

For a few minutes Laurie sat at her desk but did not go back to her homework. Instead, she chewed on a Bic pen and thought about her mother's concerns. She really was blowing it way out of proportion, wasn't she? It really was just a fad, wasn't it?

Chapter Ten

Ben Ross was having coffee in the faculty lounge when someone
came in and told him Principal Owens wanted to see him in his
office. Ross felt a tremor of nervousness. Had something gone
wrong? If Owens wanted to see him, it had to be about The Wave.

Ross stepped out into the hall and started down towards the
principal's office. On the way more than a dozen students paused
to give him The Wave salute. He returned them and continued
quickly, wondering what Owens was going to say. In one sense, if
Owens was going to tell him that there had been complaints and
that he should stop the experiment, Ross knew he would feel some
relief. Honestly, he had never expected The Wave to spread this
far. The news that kids in other classes, kids in other grades even,
had joined The Wave still amazed him. He simply hadn't intended
it to be anything like this.

And yet there was another consideration, the so-called losers in
the class – Robert Billings, for example. For the first time in his
life, Robert was an equal, a member, part of the group. No one
was making fun of him any more, no one was giving him a hard
time. And the change in Robert was indeed remarkable. Not only
had his appearance improved, but he was starting to contribute.
For the first time he was an active member of his class. And it
wasn't just history. Christy said she was noticing it in music too.
Robert seemed like a new person. To end The Wave might mean
returning Robert to the role of class creep and taking away the
only chance he had.

And wouldn't ending the experiment now also cheat the other

students who were taking part in it? Ben wondered. They would be left hanging without a chance to see where it would eventually lead them. And he would lose the chance to lead them there.

Ben abruptly stopped. Hey, wait a minute. Since when was he leading them anywhere? This was a classroom experiment, remember? An opportunity for his students to get a taste of what life in Nazi Germany might have been like. Ross smiled to himself. Let's not get carried away, he thought, and continued down the hall.

Principal Owens's door was open, and when he saw Ben Ross enter the ante-room, he motioned him in with a wave.

Ben was slightly confused. On the way down to the office he'd somehow convinced himself that Principal Owens was going to chew him out, but the old man appeared to be in a good mood.

Principal Owens was a towering man who stood over six feet four inches. His head was almost completely bald except for a few tufts of hair above either ear. His only other noteworthy feature was his pipe, always present, which protruded from his lips. He had a deep voice, and when he was angry he might instil instant religion in the most hardened atheist. But today it seemed as if Ben had nothing to fear.

Principal Owens sat behind his desk, his large black shoes propped up on one corner, and squinted slightly at Ben. 'Say, Ben, that's a good-looking suit,' he said. Owens himself had never been seen around Gordon High in less than a three-piece, even at a Saturday football game.

'Thank you, sir,' Ben replied nervously.

Principal Owens smiled. 'I can't recall seeing you in one before.'

'Uh, yes, this is something new for me,' Ben allowed.

One of the principal's eyebrows rose. 'Wouldn't have anything to do with this Wave thing, would it?'

Ben had to clear his throat. 'Well, yes it does, actually.'

Principal Owens leaned forward. 'Now, tell me, Ben, what this Wave thing is all about,' he said. 'You've got the school in a tizzy.'

'Well, I hope it's a good tizzy,' Ben Ross replied.

Principal Owens rubbed his chin. 'From what I've heard it is. Have you heard differently?'

Ben knew he had to reassure him. He quickly shook his head. 'No sir, I've heard nothing.'

The principal nodded. 'I'm all ears, Ben.'

Ben took a deep breath and began. 'It started several days ago in my senior history class. We were watching a film about the Nazis and . . .'

When he finished explaining The Wave, Ben noticed that Principal Owens looked less happy than before, but not as noticeably displeased as Ben had feared he might be. The principal removed his pipe from between his lips and tapped it on an ashtray. 'I must say it's unusual, Ben. Are you sure that the students are not falling behind?'

'If anything, they're ahead,' Ben replied.

'But there are students outside your class that are now involved with this,' the principal observed.

'But there have been no complaints,' Ben said. 'In fact Christy says she's even noticed an improvement in her classes because of it.' This was a slight exaggeration, Ben knew. But he also felt it was necessary because Owens was overreacting to The Wave.

'Still, Ben, these mottoes and this saluting bother me,' the principal said.

'It shouldn't,' Ben replied. 'It's just part of the game. And also, Norm Schiller –'

'Yes, yes, I know,' Owens said, cutting him short. 'He was in here yesterday raving about this thing. He says it's literally turned that football team of his around. The way he was talking, Ben, you would have thought he'd just drafted six future Heisman Trophy winners. Frankly, I'd just like to see them beat Clarkstown on Saturday.' The principal paused momentarily and then said, 'But that's not what I'm concerned about, Ben. I'm concerned about the students. This Wave thing seems too open-ended for my liking. I know you haven't broken any rules, but there are limits.'

'I'm completely aware of that,' Ben insisted. 'You have to understand that this experiment can't go any further than I let it go. The whole basis for The Wave is the idea of a group willing to follow their leader. And as long as I'm involved in this, I assure you it can't get out of hand.'

Principal Owens refilled his pipe with fresh tobacco and lit it, for a moment disappearing behind a small cloud of smoke while he considered Ben's words. 'Okay,' he said. 'To be perfectly frank about this, it's so different from anything we've ever had around here that I'm not sure what to think. I say, let's keep an eye on this thing, Ben. And keep your ears open too. Remember, Ben, this experiment, if that's what you want to call it, involves young, impressionable kids. Sometimes we forget that they are young and haven't developed the, uh, the judgement we hope they'll someday have. Sometimes they can take something too far if they're not watched. Understand?'

'Absolutely.'

'You promise me I'm not going to have a parade of parents down here suddenly shouting that we're indoctrinating their kids with something?'

'I promise,' Ben said.

Principal Owens nodded slightly. 'Well, I can't say that I'm crazy about this, but you've never given me cause to doubt you before.'

'And I won't now,' Ben told him.

Chapter Eleven

When Laurie Saunders got to the publications office the next day, she found a plain white envelope on the floor. Early that morning, or late the afternoon before, someone must have slipped it under the door. Laurie picked it up and closed the door behind her. Inside the envelope was a handwritten story with a note attached. Laurie read the note:

Dear Editors of *The Grapevine*,

   This is a story I have written for *The Grapevine*. Don't bother looking for my name because you won't find it. I don't want my friends or other kids to know I wrote this.

   Scowling, Laurie turned to the story. At the top of the page the anonymous author had written a title:

Welcome to the Wave – or Else

I'm a junior here at Gordon High. Three or four days ago me and my friends heard about this thing called The Wave that all the seniors were getting into. We got interested. You know how juniors always want to be like the seniors.

A bunch of us went to Mr Ross's class to see what it was. Some of my friends liked what we heard, but some of us weren't sure. It looked like a dumb game to me.

When the class was over, we started to leave. But this senior stopped us in the hall. I didn't know him, but he said he was in Mr Ross's class and asked did we want to join The Wave. Two of my friends said yes and two said they didn't know and I said I wasn't interested.

This senior started telling us how great The Wave was. He said that the more kids who joined, the better it would get. He said almost all the seniors at school had joined and most of the juniors too.

Pretty soon my two friends who said first they didn't know changed their minds and said they wanted to join. Then the senior turned to me. 'Aren't you going to stick with your friends?' he asked.

I told him they were still my friends even if I didn't join. He kept asking me why I didn't want to join. I just told him I didn't feel like it.

Then he got mad. He said pretty soon people in The Wave wouldn't want to be friends with people who weren't in it. He even said I'd lose all my friends if I didn't join. I think he was trying to scare me.

But it backfired on him. One of my friends said he didn't see why anyone had to join who didn't want to. My other friends agreed and we left.

Today I found out that three of my friends joined after some other seniors talked to them. I saw that senior from Mr Ross's class in the hall and he asked if I had joined yet. I told him I didn't intend to. He said if I didn't join soon it would be too late.

All I want to know is: Too late for what?

Laurie refolded the story and put it back in the envelope. Her thoughts about The Wave were beginning to come into focus.

As Ben left Principal Owens's office he saw several students putting up a large Wave banner in the hall. It was the day of the pep rally – the Wave rally, Ross had to remind himself. There were more students in the halls now, and he seemed to be making The Wave salute non-stop. If this kept up for much longer he was going to have one sore arm, he thought.

Further down the hall, Brad and Eric were standing at a table handing out mimeographed pamphlets and shouting, 'Strength Through Discipline, Strength Through Community, Strength Through Action.'

'Learn all about The Wave,' Brad was telling passing students. 'Here's a pamphlet.'

'And don't forget the Wave rally this afternoon,' Eric reminded them. 'Work together and achieve your goals.'

Ben smiled wearily. The untethered energy of these kids was tiring him out. There were Wave posters all over school now. Every single Wave member seemed to be involved in some activity

– recruiting new members, disseminating information, preparing the gym for the rally that afternoon. Ben found it almost overwhelming.

A little further down the hall Ben had a funny sensation and stopped. He felt as if he was being followed. A few feet behind him stood Robert, smiling. Ben smiled back and kept going, but a few seconds later he stopped again. Robert was still behind him.

'Robert, what are you doing?' Mr Ross asked.

'Mr Ross, I'm your bodyguard,' Robert announced.

'My what?'

Robert hesitated slightly. 'I want to be your bodyguard,' he said. 'I mean, you're the leader, Mr Ross; I can't let anything happen to you.'

'What could happen to me?' Ben asked, startled by the notion.

But Robert seemed to ignore that question. 'I know you need a bodyguard,' he insisted. 'I could do it, Mr Ross. For the first time in my life I feel . . . well, nobody makes jokes about me any more. I feel like I'm part of something special.'

Ben nodded.

'So can't I do it?' Robert asked. 'I know you need a bodyguard. I could do it, Mr Ross.'

Ben looked into Robert's face. Where there had once been a withdrawn and unconfident boy, there now stood a serious Wave member, concerned for his leader. But a bodyguard? Ben hesitated a moment. Wasn't that going a little too far? More and more he'd begun to recognize the position of importance his students were unconsciously forcing upon him – the ultimate leader of The Wave. Several times over the last few days he had heard Wave members discussing 'orders' he had given: orders to put posters up in the halls, orders to organize The Wave movement in the lower grades, even the order to change the pep rally into a Wave rally.

Except the crazy thing was, he'd never given those orders. Somehow they'd simply evolved in the students' imaginations, and once there, they automatically assumed he'd given them. It was as if The Wave had taken on a life of its own and now he and his students were literally riding it. Ben Ross looked at Robert Billings. Somewhere in his mind he knew that by agreeing to let Robert be his bodyguard, he was also agreeing to become a person who required a bodyguard. But wasn't that what the experiment required as well? 'All right, Robert,' he said. 'You can be my bodyguard.'

A wide smile appeared on Robert's face. Ben winked at him and continued down the hall. Perhaps having a bodyguard would be helpful. It was essential to the experiment that he maintain the image of leader of The Wave. Having a bodyguard could only enhance that image.

Chapter Twelve

The Wave rally would be in the gym, but Laurie Saunders stood by her locker, uncertain that she wanted to go. She still couldn't put into words exactly what bothered her about The Wave, but she could feel it growing inside her. Something was wrong. The anonymous letter that morning was a symptom. It wasn't only that a senior had tried to bully a junior into joining The Wave. It was more – the fact that the junior hadn't put his name on the letter, the fact that he'd been afraid to. It was something Laurie herself had been trying to deny for days, but it just wouldn't go away. The Wave was scary. Oh, it was just great if you were an unquestioning member. But if you weren't . . .

Laurie's thoughts were interrupted by a sudden flurry of shouts out in the quadrangle. She quickly went to a window and saw that two boys were fighting while a crowd of kids stood watching and yelling at them. Laurie gasped. One of the fighters was Brian Ammon! She watched as they threw punches at each other and then awkwardly wrestled to the ground. What in the world?

Now a teacher ran out and separated the two fighters. Grabbing each tightly by the arm, he started tugging them inside, no doubt to Principal Owens's office. As he went, Brian shouted, 'Strength Through Discipline! Strength Through Community! Strength Through Action!'

The other boy shouted back, 'Aw, shove it.'

'You see that?'

The sudden sound of a voice so close to her startled Laurie, and she jumped around to find David beside her.

'I hope Principal Owens lets Brian attend The Wave rally after this,' David said.

'Were they fighting about The Wave?' Laurie asked.

David shrugged. 'It's more than that. That kid Brian was fighting, he's this junior named Deutsch who's been after Brian's position all year. This thing's been brewing for weeks. I just hope he got what he deserved.'

'But Brian was shouting The Wave motto,' Laurie said.

'Well, sure. He's really into it. We all are.'

'Even the kid he was fighting?'

David shook his head. 'Naw, Deutsch is a jerk, Laurie. If he was in The Wave he wouldn't be trying to steal Brian's position. That guy's a real detriment to the team. I wish Schiller would throw him off.'

'Because he isn't in The Wave?' Laurie asked.

'Yeah,' David replied. 'If he really wanted the best for the team he'd join The Wave instead of giving Brian such a hard time. He's a one-man team, Laurie. He's just on a big ego trip and he's not helping anyone.' David looked down the hall at a clock. 'Come on, we've got to get to that rally. It's gonna start in a second.'

Suddenly Laurie made a decision. 'I'm not going,' she said.

'What?' David looked shocked. 'Why not?'

'Because I don't want to.'

'Laurie, this is an incredibly important rally,' David said. 'All the new members of The Wave are going to be there.'

'David, I think you and everyone else are taking this whole Wave thing a little bit too seriously.'

David shook his head. 'No, I'm not. You're not taking this seriously enough. Look, Laurie, you've always been a leader. The other kids, they've always looked up to you. You've got to be at that rally.'

'But that's exactly why I'm not going,' Laurie tried to explain. 'Let them make up their own minds about The Wave. They're individuals. They don't need me to help them.'

'I don't understand you,' David said.

'David, I can't believe how crazy everybody's become. The Wave is taking over everything.'

'Sure,' David said. 'Because The Wave makes sense, Laurie. It works. Everybody's on the same team. Everybody's equal for once.'

'Oh, that's terrific,' Laurie said sarcastically. 'Do we all score a touchdown?'

David stepped back and studied his girl friend. He hadn't expected anything like this. Not from Laurie.

'Don't you see,' Laurie said, mistaking his hesitation for a glimmer of doubt. 'You're so idealistic, David. You're so intent on creating some kind of utopian Wave society full of equal people and great football teams that you don't see it at all. It can't happen, David. There will always be a few people who won't want to join. They have a right not to join.'

David squinted at his girl friend. 'You know,' he said, 'you're just against this thing because you're not special any more. Because you're not the best and most popular student in the class now.'

'That's not true and you know it!' Laurie gasped.

'I think it is true!' David insisted. 'Now you know how the rest of us felt listening to you always giving the right answers. Always being the best. How does it feel not to be the best any more?'

'David, you're being stupid!' Laurie yelled at him.

David nodded. 'All right, if I'm so stupid, why don't you go find yourself a smart boyfriend.' He turned and walked away towards the gym.

Laurie stood behind and watched him. It's crazy, she thought. Everything is going out of control.

From what Laurie could hear, The Wave rally was a giant success. She was spending the period in the publications office down the hall. It was the only place she could think of going where she would be safe from the questioning looks of kids wondering why she wasn't at the rally. Laurie did not want to admit that she was hiding, but it was true. That was how crazy this whole thing had become. You had to hide if you weren't part of it.

Laurie took out a pen and chewed on it nervously. She had to do something. *The Grapevine* had to do something.

A few minutes later the turning of the doorknob shook her from her thoughts. Laurie caught her breath. Had someone come to get her?

The door opened and Alex bopped in to the beat of the music coming through his earphones.

Laurie sank back in her chair and let out a big sigh.

When Alex saw Laurie he smiled and pulled the earphones off his head. 'Hey, how come you're not in with the troops?'

Laurie shook her head. 'Alex, it's not *that* bad.'

But Alex just grinned. 'Oh yeah? Pretty soon they're gonna have to change the name of this school to Fort Gordon High.'

'I'm not amused, Alex,' Laurie said.

Alex scrunched up his shoulders and made a face. 'Laurie, you must learn that nothing is above ridicule.'

'Well, if you think they're troopers, aren't you frightened of being drafted too?' Laurie asked.

Alex grinned. 'Who, me?' Then he swiped through the air with several fierce-looking karate chops. 'Anyone hassles me and I'll kung-fu them into chopped suey.'

The door of the publications office opened again and now Carl slipped in. Seeing Laurie and Alex there, he smiled. 'Looks like I've stumbled into Anne Frank's attic,' he said.

'The last of the rugged individuals,' Alex said.

Carl nodded. 'I believe it. I just came from the rally.'

'They let you out?' Alex asked.

'I had to go to the john,' Carl answered.

'Hey, man,' Alex said. 'You got the wrong place.'

Carl grinned. 'This is where I went after the john. Anywhere but that rally.'

'Join the club,' Laurie said.

'Maybe we should give ourselves a name,' Alex said. 'If they're The Wave, we could be The Ripple.'

'What do you think?' Carl asked.

'About calling ourselves The Ripple?' Laurie said.

'No, about The Wave.'

'I think it's time we put out that issue of *The Grapevine*,' Laurie said.

'Excuse me for injecting my own not always serious opinion,' Alex said, 'but I think we ought to put it out fast before the rest of the staff gets carried away by The Mighty Wave.'

'Pass the word around to the other staff members,' Laurie said. 'On Sunday at two o'clock we'll have an emergency meeting at my house. And try to make sure only non-Wave members are there.'

That night Laurie stayed alone in her room. All afternoon she'd been too preoccupied with The Wave to allow herself to feel anything about David. Besides, they'd had fights before. But earlier in the week David had made a date to take her out that night, and here it was ten-thirty. It was obvious he wasn't coming, but Laurie couldn't quite believe it. They'd been going together since sophomore year and suddenly something as trivial as The Wave had broken them up – only The Wave wasn't trivial. Not any more.

Several times during the evening Mrs Saunders had come up to her room to ask if she wanted to talk about it, but Laurie said she didn't. Her mother was such a worry-wart, and the problem was that this time there really was something worth worrying about. Laurie had been sitting at her desk trying to write something about The Wave for *The Grapevine*, but so far the page of paper before her was empty, except for a few water marks where a tear or two had fallen.

There were knocks on her door, and Laurie quickly wiped her eyes with the palm of her hands. It was no use; if her mother came in she'd see that she was crying. 'I don't want to talk, Mom,' she said.

But the door had started to open anyway. 'It's not your mom, babe.'

'Dad?' Laurie was surprised to see her father. It wasn't that she didn't feel close to him, but unlike her mother, he usually didn't get involved in her problems. Unless they somehow concerned golf.

'Can I come in?' her father asked.

'Well, Dad,' Laurie smiled slightly, 'considering the fact that you're already in . . .'

Mr Saunders nodded. 'I'm sorry to barge in, babe, but your mother and I are both worried.'

'She told you David broke up with me?' Laurie asked.

72

'Uh, yes, she did,' Mr Saunders said. 'And I'm sorry about that, babe, I really am. I thought he was a nice boy.'

'He was,' Laurie said. Until The Wave, she thought.

'But, uh, I'm concerned about something else, Laurie. About something I heard on the golf course this evening.' Mr Saunders always left work early on Fridays to play nine holes of golf in a twilight league before the sun went down.

'What, Dad?'

'Today after school a boy was beaten up,' her father said. 'Now I got this story second-hand, so I don't know if it's all accurate. But apparently there was some kind of rally at school today, and he had resisted joining this Wave game or said something critical about it.'

Laurie was speechless.

'The boy's parents are neighbours of one of the men I play golf with. They just moved in this year. So the boy must have been new at school.'

'It sounds like he would have been a perfect candidate for joining The Wave,' Laurie said.

'Maybe,' said Mr Saunders. 'But Laurie, the boy is Jewish. Could that have had anything to do with it?'

Laurie's jaw dropped. 'You don't think ... Dad, you can't believe there's anything like that going on. I mean, I don't like The Wave, but it's not like that, Dad, I swear it isn't.'

'Are you sure?' Mr Saunders asked.

'Well, I, uh, I know everyone who was originally in The Wave. I was there when it began. The whole idea was to show how something like Nazi Germany could have happened. It wasn't for us to become little Nazis. It's . . . it's –'

'It sounds like it's got out of hand, Laurie,' her father said. 'Has it?'

Laurie just nodded. She was too shocked to be able to say anything.

'Some of the men were talking about going to the school on Monday to talk to the principal,' Mr Saunders said. 'Just, you know, to be on the safe side.'

Laurie nodded. 'We're going to put out a special issue of *The Grapevine*. We're going to expose this whole thing.'

Her father was quiet for a few moments. 'That sounds like a good idea, babe. But be careful, okay?'

'I will, Dad,' Laurie said. 'I promise.'

Chapter Thirteen

For the last three years during the football season, sitting with
Amy at Saturday afternoon games had become a habit for Laurie.
David, of course, was in the team, and while Amy didn't have a
steady boyfriend, the guys she dated were almost always football
players. By Saturday afternoon, Laurie couldn't wait to see Amy;
she had to tell her what she'd learned. It had surprised Laurie
that Amy had gone along with The Wave so far, but now Laurie
was certain that as soon as Amy learned about the boy who was
beaten up, she would quickly come to her senses. Besides, Laurie
sorely needed to talk to her about David. She still couldn't understand how something as dumb as The Wave could have made
David break up with her. Maybe Amy knew something she didn't
know. Perhaps she could even talk to David for her.

Laurie got to the game just as it was starting. It was by far the best
turnout of the year, and it took Laurie a moment to spot Amy's head
of curly blonde hair in the crowded bleachers. She was way up,
almost at the top row. Laurie hurried to an aisle and was about to start
up when someone yelled, 'Stop!'.

Laurie stopped and saw Brad coming towards her. 'Oh, hi,
Laurie, I didn't recognize you from behind,' he said. Then he
did The Wave salute.

Laurie just stood there without moving.

Brad frowned. 'Come on, Laurie, just give me the salute and
you can go up.'

'What are you talking about, Brad?'

'You know, The Wave salute.'

'You mean I can't go up into the stands unless I give The Wave salute?' Laurie asked.

Brad looked around sheepishly. 'Well, that's what they decided, Laurie.'

'Who are they?' Laurie asked.

'The Wave, Laurie, you know.'

'Brad, I thought *you* were The Wave. You're in Mr Ross's class,' Laurie said.

Brad shrugged. 'I know. Look, what's the big deal. Just give me the salute and you can go up.'

Laurie looked up at the crowded stands. 'You mean everyone in the stands gave you the salute?'

'Well, yeah. In this part of the stands.'

'Well, I want to go up and I don't want to give The Wave salute,' Laurie said angrily.

'But you can't,' Brad replied.

'Who says I can't?' Laurie asked loudly. Several students near them looked in their direction.

Brad blushed. 'Look, Laurie,' he said in a low voice. 'Just do the stupid salute now.'

But Laurie was adamant. 'No, this is ridiculous. Even you know it's ridiculous.'

Brad squirmed slightly. Then he looked around again and said, 'Okay, don't salute, just go ahead. I don't think anyone's looking.'

But all at once Laurie didn't want to join the people in the stands. She had no intention of sneaking anywhere to join The Wave. This whole thing had just gone insane. Even some of The Wave members like Brad knew it was insane. 'Brad,' she said. 'Why are you doing this if you know it's stupid? Why are you a part of it?'

'Look, Laurie, I can't talk about it now,' Brad said. 'The game's starting, I'm supposed to let people into the stands. I got too much to do.'

'Are you afraid?' Laurie asked. 'Are you afraid of what the other Wave members will do if you don't go along with them?'

Brad's mouth opened, but for a few seconds no sounds came out. 'I'm not afraid of anyone, Laurie,' he said finally. 'And you'd better shut your mouth. You know, a lot of people noticed you weren't at The Wave rally yesterday.'

'So? So what?' Laurie demanded.

'I'm not saying anything, I'm just telling you,' Brad said.

Laurie was aghast. She wanted to know what he was trying to say, but there was a big play on the field. Brad turned away, and her words were lost in the roar of the crowd.

Sunday afternoon Laurie and some of the staff of *The Grapevine* turned the Saunders' living room into a newsroom as they put together a special edition of the paper devoted almost entirely to The Wave. Several members of the newspaper were not there, and when Laurie asked those present why, they seemed reluctant to answer at first. Then Carl said, 'I have a feeling a few of our comrades would prefer not to incur the wrath of The Wave.'

Laurie looked around the room at the other staffers, who were nodding in agreement with Carl's assessment.

'Snivelling, spineless amoebas,' Alex shouted, jumping to his feet and raising his fist above his head. 'I pledge to fight The Wave until the end. Give me liberty, or give me acne!'

He looked around at the puzzled faces. 'Well,' he explained, 'I figured acne was worse than death.'

'Sit down, Alex,' someone said.

Alex sat and the group returned to the job of putting together the newspaper. But Laurie could sense that they were all acutely aware of the absent members.

The special edition on The Wave would include the story by the anonymous junior, and a report Carl had done on the sophomore who'd been beaten up.

It turned out that the boy had not been hurt badly, only roughed up by a couple of hoods. There was even some uncertainty over whether it was over The Wave, or whether The Wave was just an excuse the hoods had used to start a fight. However, one of the hoods had called the boy a dirty Jew. The boy's parents told Carl they were keeping him out of school and planned to visit Principal Owens personally Monday morning.

There were other interviews with worried parents and concerned teachers. But the most critical article was an editorial Laurie had spent most of Saturday writing. It condemned The Wave as a dangerous and mindless movement that suppressed freedom of speech and thought and ran against everything the country was founded on. She pointed out that The Wave had already begun to do more harm than good (even with The Wave, the Gordon High Gladiators had lost to Clarkstown 42 to 6) and warned that unless it was stopped it would do much worse.

Carl and Alex said they'd take the paper to the printer first thing the next morning. The paper would be out by lunchtime.

Chapter Fourteen

There was one thing Laurie had to do before the paper came out. Monday morning she had to find Amy and explain to her about the story. She still hoped that as soon as Amy read it, she would see The Wave for what it was and change her mind about it. Laurie wanted to warn her in advance so she could get out of The Wave in case there was trouble.

She found Amy in the school library and gave her a copy of the editorial to read. As Amy read, her mouth began to open wider and wider. Finally she looked up at Laurie. 'What are you going to do with it?'

'I'm publishing it in the paper,' Laurie said.

'But you can't say these things about The Wave,' Amy said.

'Why not?' Laurie asked. 'They're true. Amy, The Wave has become an obsession with everyone. No one is thinking for themselves any more.'

'Oh, come on, Laurie,' Amy said. 'You're just upset. You're letting your fight with David get to you.'

Laurie shook her head. 'Amy, I'm serious. The Wave is hurting people. And everyone's going along with it like a flock of sheep. I can't believe that after reading this you'd still be part of it. Don't you see what The Wave is? It's everybody forgetting who they are. It's like *Night of the Living Dead* or something. Why do you want to be part of it?'

'Because it means that nobody is better than anyone else for once,' Amy said. 'Because ever since we became friends all I've ever done is try to compete with you and keep up with you. But now I don't feel like I have to have a boyfriend on the football team like you. And if I don't want to, I don't have to get the same grades you get, Laurie. For the first time in three years I feel like I don't have to keep up with Laurie Saunders and people will still like me.'

Laurie felt chills run down her arms. 'I, I, uh, always knew you felt that way,' she stammered. 'I always wanted to talk to you about it.'

'Don't you know that half the parents in school say to their kids, "Why can't you be like Laurie Saunders?"' Amy asked. 'Come on, Laurie, the only reason you're against The Wave is because it means you're not a princess any more.'

Laurie was stunned. Even her best friend, someone as smart as Amy, was turning against her because of The Wave. It made her angry. 'Well, I'm publishing this,' she said.

Amy only looked up at her and said, 'Don't, Laurie.'

But Laurie shook her head. 'I already have,' she said. 'And I know what I have to do.'

Suddenly it was as if she was a stranger. Amy looked at her watch. 'I gotta go,' she said, and walked away, leaving Laurie standing alone in the library.

Copies of *The Grapevine* had never been scooped up faster than they were that day. The school was abuzz with the news. Very few kids had heard about the sophomore who was beaten up, and of course no one had heard the story by the anonymous junior before. But as soon as those stories appeared in the paper, other stories began to circulate. Stories of threats and abuse directed at kids who, for one reason or another, had resisted The Wave.

There were other rumours going around too, that teachers and parents had been to Principal Owens's office all morning complaining, and that the school counsellors had begun interviewing students. There was an air of unease in the halls and classrooms.

In the faculty lounge, Ben Ross put down his copy of *The Grapevine* and rubbed his temples with his fingers. Suddenly he'd got a terrible headache. Something had gone wrong and somewhere in his mind Ross suspected that he was to blame for it. The roughing up of this boy was terrible, unbelievable. How could he justify an experiment that had such effects?

He was also surprised to find himself disturbed by the football team's embarrassing defeat by Clarkstown. It seemed odd to him that although he didn't care the least about high school athletics, this defeat would bother him so. Was it because of The Wave? During the last week he had begun to believe that if the football team fared well it would be a strong argument for the success of The Wave.

But since when did he want The Wave to succeed? The success or failure of The Wave was not the point of the experiment. He was supposed to be interested in what his students learned from The Wave, not in The Wave itself.

There was a medicine chest in the faculty lounge, stocked with just about every brand of aspirin and non-aspirin headache remedy that had ever been invented. A friend of his had once remarked that while doctors as a group suffered from the highest incidence of suicide, teachers had to have the highest incidence of headaches. Ben shook three tablets from a bottle and headed for the door to get some water.

But just as he reached the faculty room door, Ben stopped. Outside in the hall he could hear voices – Norm Schiller's and another male voice he didn't recognize. Someone must have stopped Norm just as he was going into the faculty lounge and now he stood outside the door talking. Ben listened from inside.

'No, it wasn't worth a damn,' Schiller was saying. 'Sure it got them psyched up, made 'em think they could win. But out on the field they couldn't execute. All the waves in the world don't mean a thing next to a well-executed quarterback option. There's no substitute for learning the damn game.'

'Ross really has these kids brainwashed if you ask me,' the unidentified man said. 'I don't know what the hell he thinks he's up to, but I don't like it. And none of the other teachers I've talked to do either. Where does he get the right?'

'Don't ask me,' Schiller said.

The faculty room door began to open and Ben quickly backed away, pushing through a door into the small faculty bathroom that adjoined the lounge. His heart was pounding rapidly and his head hurt even more. He swallowed the three aspirins and avoided looking at himself in the mirror. Was he afraid of who he might see? A high school history teacher who had accidentally slipped into the role of a dictator?

David Collins still couldn't understand it. It didn't make sense to him why everyone hadn't joined The Wave in the first place. Then there never would have been these hassles. They all could have functioned as equals, as team-mates. People were laughing and saying that The Wave didn't help the football team at all on Saturday, but what did they expect? The Wave wasn't a miracle drug. The team had known about The Wave for exactly five days before the game. What had changed was the team spirit and the team attitude.

David stood outside on the school lawn with Robert Billings and a bunch of other kids from Mr Ross's class looking at *The Grapevine*. Laurie's story made him feel a little sick. He hadn't heard anything about anyone threatening or hurting anyone and for all he knew, she and her staff had made it all up. An unsigned letter and a story about a sophomore he'd never heard of. Okay, he was unhappy that Laurie refused to be part of The Wave. But why couldn't she and the people like her just leave The Wave alone? Why did they have to attack it?

Robert, beside him, was getting really upset over Laurie's story. 'These are all lies,' he said angrily. 'She can't be allowed to say these things.'

'It's not that important,' David told him. 'Nobody cares what Laurie's writing or what she has to say.'

'Are you kidding?' Robert said. 'Anyone who reads this is going to get the completely wrong idea about The Wave.'

'I told her not to publish it,' Amy said.

'Hey, relax,' David said. 'There's no law that says people have to believe in what we're trying to do. But if we can keep making The Wave work, they'll see. They'll see all the good things it can do.'

'Yeah, but if we don't watch out,' Eric said, 'these people are going to ruin it for the rest of us. Have you heard the rumours going around today? I heard there are parents and teachers and all kinds of people in Principal Owens's office complaining. Can you believe that? At this rate no one will get a chance to see what The Wave can do.'

'Laurie Saunders is a threat,' Robert stated bluntly. 'She must be stopped.'

David didn't like the sinister tone in Robert's voice. 'Hey, wait –' he began to protest.

But Brian cut him off. 'Don't worry, Robert, David and I can take care of Laurie, right, Dave?'

'Uh . . .' David suddenly felt Brian's hand on his shoulder slowly guiding him away from the rest of the group. Robert was nodding in approval.

'Look, man,' Brian whispered. 'If anyone can get Laurie to stop, you can.'

'Yea, but I don't like Robert's attitude,' David hissed back. 'It's like we must wipe out anyone who resists us. That's the exact opposite of how we should approach this.'

'Dave, listen. Robert is just a little over-enthusiastic sometimes. But you have to admit he has a point. If Laurie keeps writing stuff like this, The Wave won't have a chance. Just tell her to cool it, Dave. She'll listen to you.'

'I don't know, Brian.'

'Look, we'll wait for her after school tonight. Then you can go talk to her, okay?'

David nodded reluctantly. 'I guess.'

Chapter Fifteen

Christy Ross was in a hurry to get home after choir that afternoon. Ben had disappeared from school half-way through the day, and she had a feeling she knew why. When she got home she found her husband hunched over a book on Nazi youth. 'What happened to you today?' she asked.

Without looking up from his book, Ben answered irritably, 'I left early. I, uh, wasn't feeling well. But I need to be alone now, Chris. I have to be prepared for tomorrow.'

'But honey, I need to talk to you,' Christy implored.

'Can't it wait?' Ben snapped. 'I've got to finish this before class tomorrow.'

'No,' Christy insisted. 'That's what I have to talk to you about. This Wave thing. Have you any idea what's going on at school, Ben? I mean, let's not even dwell on the fact that half my class has been skipping just to go to yours. Do you realize that this Wave of yours is disrupting the entire school? At least three teachers stopped me in the hall today to ask what the hell you're up to. And they're complaining to the principal too.'

'I know, I know. And that's because they just don't understand what I'm trying to do,' Ben answered.

'Are you serious, Ben?' his wife asked. 'Did you know that the school counsellors have begun questioning students in your class?' his wife asked. 'Are you sure *you* know what you're doing? Because frankly, no one else in school thinks you do.'

'Don't you think I know that?' Ben replied. 'I know what

they're saying about me. That I'm crazy with power . . . that I'm on an ego trip.'

'Have you thought that they may be right?' Christy asked. 'I mean, think of your original goals. Are they still the same ones you have now?'

Ben ran his hands through his hair. He already had enough problems with The Wave. 'Christy, I thought you were on my side.' But inside, he knew that she was right.

'I am on your side, Ben,' his wife answered. 'But I've seen you these last few days and it's as if I don't even know you. You've become so involved in playing this role at school that you're starting to slip into it at home. I've seen you go overboard like this before, Ben. Now you've got to turn it off, honey.'

'I know. It must look to you like I've gone too far. But I can't stop now.' He shook his head wearily. 'Not yet.'

'Then when?' Christy asked angrily. 'After you or some of these kids do something you'll all regret?'

'Do you think I'm not aware of that?' Ben asked. 'Do you think it doesn't worry me? But I created this experiment, and they went along. If I stop now they'll all be left hanging. They'd be confused, and they wouldn't have learned anything.'

'Well, let them be confused,' Christy said.

Ben suddenly jumped to his feet in frustrated anger. 'No, I won't do that. I can't do that!' he shouted at his wife. 'I'm their teacher. I was responsible for getting them into this. I admit that maybe I did let this go too long. But they've come too far to just drop it now. I have to push them until they get the point. I might be teaching these kids the most important lesson of their lives!'

Christy was not impressed. 'Well, I just hope Principal Owens agrees with you, Ben,' she told him. 'Because he caught me as I was leaving today and said he'd been looking for you all day. He wants to see you first thing tomorrow morning.'

The Grapevine staff stayed late after school that day to celebrate their victory. The issue on The Wave had been so successful that it was almost impossible to find an extra copy anywhere. Not only that, but teachers and administrators and even some students had been stopping them all day and thanking them for revealing 'the other side' of The Wave. Already they had heard stories that some students were resigning from The Wave.

The staff had realized that a single issue of the paper was not enough to stop a movement that had gained as much momentum as The Wave had that past week. But at least they had struck it a serious blow. Carl said he doubted there would be any more incidents of threats against non-Wave members – or any more beatings.

As usual Laurie was the last one to leave the publications office. One thing about *The Grapevine* staff – they were great at parties, but when it became time to clean up somehow they all disappeared. It had come as a shock to Laurie earlier that year when she realized what having the top position on the paper, editor-in-chief, really meant: having to do every little stupid job no one else wanted to do. And tonight that meant cleaning up after the rest of the staff went home.

By the time she finished, Laurie realized that it had already grown dark out, and she was practically alone in the school building. As she closed the door of *The Grapevine* office and turned off the light, that nervousness she'd felt all week began to return again. The Wave was undoubtedly smarting from the wounds *The Grapevine* had inflicted, but it was still strong in Gordon High, and Laurie was aware that as the head of the paper, she . . . no, she told herself, you're just being silly and paranoid. The Wave was nothing serious, just a classroom experiment that had got slightly out of hand. There was nothing to be afraid of.

The corridors were darkened now as Laurie headed to her locker to drop off a book she would not need that evening. The silence of the empty school was eerie. For the first time she heard sounds she'd never heard before: the hums and buzzes of electrical current running to and from alarms and smoke detectors. A bubbling, splashing sound coming from the science room where some overnight experiment must have been left brewing. Even the unusually loud, hollow echo of her own shoes as they rapped the hard corridor floors.

A few feet from her locker, Laurie froze. There on her locker door, the word 'enemy' was painted in red letters. Suddenly the loudest noise in the corridor was the quick, insistent beating of her own heart. Calm down, she told herself. Someone is just trying to scare you. She tried to get control of herself and started to do the combination of her lock. But she stopped in mid-turn. Had she heard something? Footsteps?

Laurie backed slowly away from her locker, gradually losing her battle to suppress her own growing fright. She turned and started walking down the hallway towards the exit. The sound of footsteps seemed to be growing louder, and Laurie quickened her pace. The footsteps grew even louder, and all at once the lights at the far end of the hall went out. Terrified, Laurie turned and peered back down into the dark hallway. Was that someone? Was there someone down there?

The next thing Laurie knew she was running down the hallway towards the exit doors at the end. It seemed to take forever to get there, and when she finally reached the double metal doors and banged her hip against the opening bar, they were locked!

In a panic, Laurie threw herself against the next set of doors. Miraculously they opened, and she flew out into the cool evening air, running and running.

It seemed as if she ran for a long time, and finally she lost her breath and had to slow down, clutching her books to her breast and breathing hard. She felt safer now.

David sat waiting in the passenger seat of Brian's van. They were parked near the all-night tennis courts because David knew that when Laurie came home from school after dark she always took this route, where the bright lights from the courts made her feel safe. For almost an hour now they had been sitting in the van. Brian was in the driver's seat, keeping his eye on the sideview mirror watching for Laurie, and whistling some song so out of tune that David had no idea what it was. David watched the tennis players and listened to the monotonous plunk-ka-plunk of tennis balls being hit back and forth.

'Brian, can I ask you a question?' David said after a long while. 'What?'

'What are you whistling?'

Brian seemed surprised. ' "Take Me Out to the Ball Game",'

he said. Then he whistled a few more bars. Coming from his lips, the song seemed completely unrecognizable. 'There, now can you tell?'

David nodded. 'Sure, Brian, sure.' He went back to watching the tennis players.

A moment later, Brian sat up in his seat. 'Hey, here she comes.'

David turned and looked down the block. Laurie was coming down the path, walking quickly. He reached for the door handle. 'Okay, now just let me take care of this alone,' he said, pulling the handle.

'Just as long as she understands,' Brian said. 'We're not playing around any more.'

'Sure, Brian,' David said and got out of the van. Now Brian was starting to sound like Robert too.

He had to jog to catch up with her, all the while uncertain of how he should handle this. All he knew was that it was better that he do it than Brian. He reached her, but Laurie did not stop, and he had to walk quickly to keep up with her.

'Hey, Laurie, can't you wait up?' he asked. 'I've got to talk to you. It's really important.'

Laurie slowed down and glanced behind him.

'It's okay, nobody else is coming,' David said.

Laurie stopped. David noticed she was breathing hard and clutching her books tightly.

'Well, David,' she said. 'I'm not used to seeing you alone. Where are your troops?'

David knew he had to ignore her antagonistic remarks and try to reason with her. 'Look, Laurie, will you just listen to me for a minute, please?'

But Laurie didn't seem interested. 'David, we said everything we had to say to each other the other day. I don't want to rehash it now, so just leave me alone.'

Against his will, David felt himself getting mad. She wouldn't even listen. 'Laurie, you've got to stop writing stuff against The Wave. You're causing all kinds of problems.'

'The Wave is causing the problems, David.'

'It is not,' David insisted. 'Look, Laurie, we want you with us, not against us.'

Laurie shook her head. 'Well, count me out. I told you, I quit. This is not a game any more. People have been hurt.'

She started to walk away, but David followed her. 'That was an accident,' he insisted. 'Some guys just used The Wave as an excuse for beating that kid up. Don't you see? The Wave is still for the good of the whole. Why can't you see that, Laurie? It could be a whole new system. We could make it work.'

'Not with me, you can't.'

David knew if he didn't stop her she'd get away. It just wasn't fair that one person could ruin it for everyone else. He had to convince her. He had to! The next thing he knew, he had grabbed her arm.

'Let go of me!' Laurie struggled to get free, but David held her arm tightly.

'Laurie, you've got to stop,' he said. It just wasn't fair.

'David, let go of my arm!'

'Laurie, stop writing those articles! Keep your mouth shut about The Wave! You're ruining it for everyone else!'

But Laurie kept resisting. 'I will write and I will say anything that I want to, and you can't stop me!' she yelled at him.

Overcome with anger, David grabbed her other arm. Why did she have to be so stubborn? Why couldn't she see how good The Wave could be? 'We can stop you, and we will!' he shouted at her.

But Laurie only struggled harder to get out of his grasp. 'I hate you!' she cried. 'I hate The Wave! I hate all of you!'

The words struck David like a hard slap in the face. Almost out of control, he screamed 'Shut up!' and threw her down on the grass. Her books went flying as she fell roughly to the ground.

David instantly recoiled in shock at what he had done. Laurie lay still on the ground and he was filled with fear as he dropped to his knees and put his arms around her. 'Jeez, Laurie, are you all right?'

Laurie nodded, but seemed unable to talk as sobs filled her throat.

David held her tightly. 'God, I'm sorry,' he whispered. He could feel her tremble and he wondered how on earth he could have done something so stupid. What could have made him want to hurt the girl, the one he really still loved. Laurie pushed herself up slightly and sat sobbing and gasping for breath. David could not believe it. He felt almost as if he were coming out of a trance. What had possessed him these last days that could cause him to do something so stupid? There he'd been, denying that The Wave could hurt anyone, and at the same time he'd hurt Laurie, his own girl friend, in the name of The Wave!

It was crazy – but David knew that he'd been wrong. Anything that could make him do what he'd just done was wrong. It had to be.

Meanwhile, moving slowly down the street, Brian's van passed them and disappeared into the darkness.

Later that night, Christy Ross went into the study where her husband was working. 'Ben,' she said firmly, 'I'm sorry to interrupt you, but I've been thinking, and I have something important to say.'

Ben leaned back in his chair and looked at his wife uneasily.

'Ben, you've got to end The Wave tomorrow,' Christy told him. 'I know how much this means to you and how important you think it is for your students. But I'm telling you it must end.'

'How can you say that?' Ben asked.

'Because, Ben, if you don't end it I am convinced Principal Owens will,' she told him. 'And if he has to end it, I promise you your experiment will be a failure. I've been thinking all evening about what you've been trying to accomplish, Ben, and I think I'm beginning to understand. But did you ever consider, back when you began this experiment, what might happen if it didn't work? Did it ever occur to you that you're risking your reputation as a teacher? If this goes wrong, do you think parents are going to let their kids into your classroom again?'

'Don't you think you're exaggerating?' Ben asked.

'No,' Christy replied. 'Did it ever occur to you that you've not only put yourself into jeopardy but me as well? Some people think that just because I'm your wife that somehow I'm involved in this Wave idiocy too. Does that seem fair, Ben? It breaks my heart that after two years at Gordon High you're in danger of ruining your job. You're going to end it tomorrow, Ben. You're going to go into Principal Owens and tell him that it's over.'

'Christy, how can you tell me what to do?' Ben asked. 'How can I possibly end it in one day and still do the students justice?'

'You have to think of something, Ben,' Christy insisted. 'You just have to.'

Ben rubbed his forehead and thought about the next morning's meeting with Principal Owens. Owens was a good man, and open to new ideas and experiments, but now he had immense pressures on him. On one side parents and teachers were up in arms over The Wave, and pressure was growing on the Principal to step in and put a halt to it. On the other side there was only Ben Ross, pleading with him not to interfere, trying to explain that to stop The Wave abruptly could be a disaster for the students. So much effort had gone into it. To end The Wave without explanation would be like reading the first half of a novel and not finishing it. But Christy was right. Ben knew The Wave had to end. The important thing wasn't when it ended, but how. The students had to end it themselves, and they had to understand why. Otherwise the lesson, the pain, all that had gone into it, was for nothing.

'Christy,' Ben said, 'I know it should end, but I just don't see how.'

His wife sighed wearily. 'Are you saying that you're going to go into Principal Owens's office tomorrow morning and tell *him* that? That you know it should end but you don't know how? Ben, you're supposed to be The Wave's leader. You're the one they're supposed to follow blindly.'

Ben did not appreciate the sarcasm in his wife's voice, but again he knew she was right. The students in The Wave had made him more of a leader than he had ever wished to be. But it was also true that he had not resisted. In fact, he had to admit that before the experiment had gone bad, he had enjoyed those fleeting moments of power. A crowded room full of students obeying his commands, the Wave symbol he'd created posted all over the school, even a bodyguard. He had read that power could be seductive, and now he had experienced it. Ben ran his hand through his hair. The members of The Wave were not the only ones who had to learn the lesson power taught. Their teacher did, as well.

'Ben?' Christy said.

'Yes, I know, I'm thinking,' he replied. Wondering was more like it. Suppose there was something he could do tomorrow. Suppose he did something abrupt and final. Would they follow him? At once, Ben understood what he had to do. 'Okay, Christy, I've got an idea.'

His wife looked at him uncertainly. 'Something you're sure will work?'

Ben shook his head. 'No, but I hope it will,' he said.

Christy nodded and looked at her watch. It was late and she was tired. She leaned over her husband and kissed him on the forehead. The skin was damp with perspiration. 'You coming to bed?'

'Soon,' he said.

After Christy went into the bedroom, Ben went over his plan again in his mind. It seemed sound and he stood up, determined to get some sleep. He was just shutting off the lights when the doorbell rang. Rubbing his eyes with weariness, Ross trudged to the front door.

'Who is it?'

'It's David Collins and Laurie Saunders, Mr Ross.'

Surprised, Ben pulled the door open. 'What are you doing here?' he asked. 'It's late.'

'Mr Ross, we've got to talk to you,' David said. 'It's really important.'

'Well, come in and sit down,' Ben said.

As David and Laurie entered the living room, Ben could see that both of them were shaken up. Had something even worse happened because of The Wave? God forbid. The two students sat down on the couch. David leaned forward.

'Mr Ross, you've got to help us,' he said, his voice filled with agitation.

'What is it?' Ben asked. 'What's wrong?'

'It's The Wave,' David said.

'Mr Ross,' said Laurie, 'we know how important this is to you – but it's just gone too far.'

Before Ross could even respond, David added, 'It's taken over, Mr Ross. You can't say anything against it. People are afraid to.'

'The kids at school are scared,' Laurie told him. 'They're really scared. Not only to say anything against The Wave, but of what might happen to them if they don't go along with it.'

Ben nodded. In a way, what these students were telling him relieved him of part of his concern about The Wave. If he did as Christy told him and thought back to the original goals of the experiment, then the fears Laurie and David spoke of confirmed that The Wave was a success. After all, The Wave had originally been conceived as a way to show these kids what life in Nazi Germany might have been like. Apparently, in terms of fear and forced compliance, it had been an overwhelming success – too much of a success.

'You can't even have a conversation without wondering who's listening,' Laurie told him.

Ben could only nod again. He recalled those students in his own history classes who had condemned the Jews for not taking the Nazi threat seriously, for not fleeing their homes and ghettos when rumours of the concentration camps and gas chambers first filtered back to them. Of course, Ross thought, how could any rational person believe such a thing? And who could have believed that a nice bunch of high school students like those at Gordon High could have become a fascist group called The Wave? Was it a weakness of man that made him want to ignore the darker side of his fellow human beings?

David yanked him from his thoughts. 'Tonight I almost hurt Laurie because of The Wave,' he said. 'I don't know what came over me. But I do know that it's the same thing that's come over almost everyone who's in The Wave.'

'You've got to stop it,' Laurie urged him.

'I know,' Ben said. 'I will.'

'What are you going to do, Mr Ross?' David asked.

Ben knew he could not reveal his plan to Laurie and David. It was essential that the members of The Wave decide the matter for themselves, and for the experiment to be a true success, Ben could only present them with the evidence. If David or Laurie went to school the next day and told the students that Mr Ross planned to end The Wave, the students would be biased. They might end it without really understanding why it had to end. Or worse, they might try and fight him, keeping The Wave alive despite its obvious destiny.

'David, Laurie,' he said, 'you have discovered for yourselves what the other members of The Wave have not yet learned. I promise you that tomorrow I will try to help them towards that discovery. But I have to do it my way, and I can only ask that you trust me. Can you do that?'

David and Laurie nodded uncertainly as Ben rose and showed them to the door. 'Come on, it's too late for you kids to be out,' he told them. As they went through the door, however, Ben had another thought. 'Listen, do either of you know two students who have never been involved in The Wave? Two students who Wave members don't know and wouldn't miss?'

David considered for a moment. Amazing as it might be, almost everyone he knew in school had become a member of The Wave. But Laurie thought of two people. 'Alex Cooper and Carl Block,' she said. 'They're on *The Grapevine* staff.'

'Okay,' Ben told them. 'Now, I want both of you to go back to class tomorrow and act as if everything is fine. Pretend we haven't talked, and don't tell anyone that you were here tonight or that you spoke to me. Can you do that?'

David nodded, but Laurie looked concerned. 'I don't know, Mr Ross.'

But Ben cut her short. 'Laurie, it is extremely important that we do it this way. You must trust me. Okay?'

Reluctantly Laurie agreed. Ben bade them good-bye, and she and David stepped into the dark.

Chapter Sixteen

The next morning in Principal Owens's office, Ben had to pull his handkerchief out of his pocket and pat the perspiration off his forehead. Across the desk, Principal Owens had just slammed his fist down. 'Damn it, Ben! I don't care about your experiment. I've got teachers complaining, I've got parents calling me every five minutes wanting to know what the hell's going on here, what the hell are we doing with their kids. You think I can tell *them* it's an experiment? My God, man, you know that boy who was roughed up last week? His rabbi was here yesterday. The man spent two years in Auschwitz. Do you think he gives a damn about your experiment?'

Ben sat up in his chair. 'Principal Owens, I understand the pressure you're under. I know that The Wave went too far. I . . .' Ben took a deep breath. 'I realize now that I made a mistake. A history class is not a science lab. You can't experiment with human beings. Especially high school students who aren't aware that they're part of an experiment. But for a moment let's forget that it was a mistake, that it went too far. Let's look at it right now. Right now there are two hundred students here who think The Wave is great. I can still teach them a lesson. All I need is the rest of the day, and I can teach them a lesson they will never forget.'

Principal Owens looked at him sceptically. 'And what do you expect me to tell their parents and the other teachers in the meantime?'

Ben patted his forehead with his handkerchief again. He knew he was taking a gamble, but what choice did he have? He had got them into this and he had to get them out. 'Tell them that I promise it will all be over by tonight.'

Principal Owens arched an eyebrow. 'And exactly how do you intend to do that?'

It didn't take Ben long to outline his plan. Across the desk, Principal Owens tapped out his pipe and considered it. A long and uncomfortable silence followed. Finally he said, 'Ben, I'm going to be absolutely straight with you. This Wave thing has made Gordon High look very bad, and I'm very unhappy about it. I'll let you have today. But I have to warn you: if it doesn't work, I'm going to have to ask you for your resignation.'

Ben nodded. 'I understand,' he said.

Principal Owens stood and offered his hand. 'I hope you can make this work, Ben,' he said solemnly. 'You're a fine teacher and we'd hate to lose you.'

Outside in the hall Ben had no time to dwell on Principal Owens's words. He had to find Alex Cooper and Carl Block, and he had to work fast.

In history class that day Ben waited until the students had come to attention. Then he said, 'I have a special announcement about The Wave. At five o'clock today there will be a rally in the auditorium – for Wave members only.'

David smiled to himself and winked at Laurie.

'The reason for the rally is the following,' Mr Ross continued. 'The Wave is not just a classroom experiment. It's much, much more than that. Unknown to you, starting last week, all across the country teachers like myself have been recruiting and training a youth brigade to show the rest of the nation how to achieve a better society.

'As you know, this country has just gone through a decade in which steady double-digit inflation has severely weakened the economy,' Mr Ross continued. 'Unemployment has run chronically high, and the crime rate has been worse than any time in memory. Never before has the morale of the United States been so low. Unless this trend is stopped, a growing number of people, including the founders of The Wave, believe that our country is doomed.'

David was no longer smiling. This was not what he had expected to hear. Mr Ross didn't seem to be ending The Wave at all. If anything, he seemed to be going more deeply into it than ever!

'We must prove that through discipline, community, and action we can turn this country around,' Ross told the class. 'Look what we have accomplished in this school alone in just a few days. If we can change things here, we can change things everywhere.'

Laurie gave David a frightened look. Mr Ross went on: 'In factories, hospitals, universities – in all institutions –'

David jumped out of his chair in protest. 'Mr Ross, Mr Ross!'

'Sit down, David!' Mr Ross ordered.

'But, Mr Ross, you said –'

Ben cut him off urgently. 'I said, sit down, David. Don't interrupt me.'

David returned to his seat, unable to believe his ears as Mr Ross continued: 'Now listen carefully. During the rally the founder and national leader of The Wave will appear on cable television to announce the formation of a National Wave Youth Movement!'

All around them students started cheering. It was too much for Laurie and David. Both rose to their feet, this time to face the class.

'Wait, wait,' David pleaded with them. 'Don't listen to him. Don't listen. He's lying.'

'Can't you scc what he's doing?' Laurie said emotionally. 'Can't any of you think for yourselves any more?'

But the room only grew quiet as the class glared at them.

Ross knew he had to act quickly, before Laurie and David revealed too much. He realized he had made an error. He had asked Laurie and David to trust him, and he had not expected them to disobey. But instantly it made sense to him that they would. He snapped his fingers. 'Robert, I want you to take over the class until I return from escorting David and Laurie to the Principal's office.'

'Mr Ross, yes!'

Mr Ross quickly walked to the classroom door and held it open for Laurie and David.

Outside in the hall, David and Laurie walked slowly towards the

Principal's office, followed by Mr Ross. In the background they could hear steady, loud chants emanating from Mr Ross's room: 'Strength Through Discipline! Strength Through Community! Strength Through Action!'

'Mr Ross, you lied to us last night,' David said bitterly.

'No, I didn't, David. But I told you, you would have to trust me,' Mr Ross replied.

'Why should we?' Laurie asked. 'You were the one who started The Wave in the first place.'

The point was a good one. Ben could think of no reason why they should trust him. He only knew that they should. He hoped that by evening they would understand.

David and Laurie spent most of the afternoon waiting outside Principal Owens's office to see him. They were miserable and depressed, certain that Mr Ross had tricked them into co-operating with him so that they could not prevent what now appeared to be the final hours before The Wave movement at Gordon High joined the national Wave movement, which had been growing simultaneously at high schools all over the country.

Even Principal Owens seemed unsympathetic when he finally got around to seeing them. On his desk was a brief report from Mr Ross, and although neither of them could see what it said, it was obvious that it must have stated that Laurie and David had disrupted the class. Both of them pleaded with the Principal to stop The Wave and the five o'clock rally, but Principal Owens only insisted that everything would be all right.

Finally he told them to go back to their classes. David and Laurie were incredulous. Here they were trying to prevent the worst thing they'd ever seen happen in school and Principal Owens seemed to be oblivious.

Out in the hall, David threw his books into his locker and slammed the door shut. 'Forget it,' he told Laurie angrily. 'I'm not hanging around here any more today. I'm splitting.'

'Just wait for me to put my books away,' Laurie told him. 'I'll join you.'

A few minutes later, as they walked down the path away from

school, Laurie sensed that David was getting depressed. 'I can't believe how dumb I was, Laurie,' he kept saying. 'I can't believe I really fell for it.'

Laurie squeezed his hand. 'You weren't dumb, David. You were idealistic. I mean, there were good things about The Wave. It couldn't be all bad, or no one would have joined in the first place. It's just that they don't see what's bad about it. They think it makes everyone equal, but they don't understand that it robs you of your right to be independent.'

'Laurie, is it possible that we're wrong about The Wave?' David asked.

'No, David, we're right,' Laurie answered.

'Then why doesn't anybody else see it?' he asked.

'I don't know. It's like they're all in a trance. They just won't listen any more.'

David nodded hopelessly.

It was still early and they decided to walk to a park near by. Neither wanted to go home yet. David wasn't sure what to think of The Wave or Mr Ross. Laurie still believed it was a fad that the kids would ultimately get bored with, no matter who organized it or where. What frightened her was what the kids in The Wave might do before they grew tired of it.

'I feel alone all of a sudden,' David said as they walked through the trees in the park. 'It's like all my friends are part of a crazy movement and I'm an outcast just because I refuse to be exactly like them.'

Laurie knew exactly how he felt, because she felt it too. She moved close to him and he put his arm around her. Laurie felt closer to David than ever. Wasn't it odd how going through something bad like this could bring them closer? She thought back to the night before, how David had forgotten entirely about The Wave the second he'd realized he'd hurt her. Suddenly she hugged him hard.

'What?' David was surprised.

'Oh, uh, nothing,' she said.

'Hmmm.' David looked away.

Laurie felt her mind drifting back to The Wave. She tried to imagine the school auditorium that afternoon, filled with Wave members. And some leader somewhere speaking to them over the television. What would he tell them? To burn books? To force all non-Wave members to wear armbands? It seemed so utterly crazy that anything like this could happen. So . . . suddenly Laurie remembered something. 'David,' she said, 'do you remember the day this all started?'

'The day Mr Ross taught us the first motto?' David asked.

'No, David, the day before that – the day we saw that movie about the Nazi concentration camps. The day I was so upset. Remember? No one could understand how all the other Germans could have ignored what the Nazis were doing and pretended they didn't know.'

'Yeah?' David said.

Laurie looked up at him. 'David, do you remember what you said to me at lunch that afternoon?'

David tried to recall for a moment, but then shook his head.

'You told me it could never happen again.'

David looked at her for a second. He felt himself smiling ironically. 'You know something?' he said. 'Even with the meeting with that national leader at the rally this afternoon – even though I was part of it, I still can't believe it's happening. It's so insane.'

'I was just thinking the same thing,' Laurie said. Then an idea struck her. 'David, let's go back to school.'

'Why?'

'I want to see him,' she said. 'I want to see this leader. I swear, I won't believe this is really happening until I see it for myself.'

'But Mr Ross said it was for Wave members only.'

'What do you care?' Laurie asked him.

David shrugged. 'I don't know, Laurie. I don't know if I want to go back. I feel like . . . like The Wave got me once and if I go back it might get me again.'

'No way,' Laurie laughed.

Chapter Seventeen

It was incredible, Ben Ross thought as he walked towards the auditorium. Ahead of him, two of his students sat at a small table in front of the auditorium doors, checking membership cards. Wave members were streaming into the auditorium, many carrying Wave banners and signs. Ross couldn't help thinking that before the advent of The Wave it would have taken a week to organize so many students. Today it had taken only a few hours. He sighed. So much for the positive side of discipline, community, and action. He wondered, if he was successful in 'de-programming' the students from The Wave, how long it would be before he'd begin seeing sloppy homework again. He smiled. Is this the price we pay for freedom?

As Ben watched, Robert, wearing a jacket and tie, came out of the auditorium and exchanged salutes with Brad and Brian.

'The auditorium is full,' Robert told them. 'Are the guards in place?'

'They are,' Brad said.

Robert looked pleased. 'Okay, let's check all the doors. Make sure they're all locked.'

Ben rubbed his hands together nervously. It was time to go in. He walked towards the stage entrance and noticed that Christy was there waiting for him.

'Hi.' She kissed him quickly on the cheek. 'I thought I'd wish you luck.'

'Thanks, I'll need it,' Ben said.

Christy straightened his tie. 'Did anyone ever tell you you look great in suits?' she asked.

'Matter of fact, Owens said that the other day.' Ben sighed. 'If I have to start looking for a new job, I might be wearing them a lot.'

'Don't worry. You'll do fine,' Christy told him.

Ben managed a slight smile. 'I wish I had your faith in me,' he said.

Christy laughed and turned him towards the stage door. 'Go get 'em, tiger.'

The next thing Ben knew, he was standing near the side of the stage, looking out at the crowded auditorium filled with Wave members. A moment later Robert joined him there.

'Mr Ross,' he said, saluting, 'all the doors are secure and the guards are in place.'

'Thank you, Robert,' Ben said.

It was time to begin. As he strode to the centre of the auditorium stage, Ben glanced quickly towards the curtains behind him and then up at the projectionist's booth at the back of the room. As he stopped and stood between two large television monitors that had been ordered from the A V department that day, the crowd burst spontaneously into The Wave mottoes, standing at their seats and giving The Wave salute.

'Strength Through Discipline!'

'Strength Through Community!'

'Strength Through Action!'

Before them, Ben stood motionless. When they had finished their chants, he held up his arms for silence. In an instant the huge roomful of students went silent. Such obedience, Ben thought sadly. He looked out over the large crowd, aware that this was probably the last time he would be able to hold their attention so firmly. Then he spoke.

'In a moment our national leader will address us.' And turning he said, 'Robert.'

'Mr Ross, yes.'

'Turn on the television sets.'

Robert turned on both sets and the picture tubes grew bright and blue, with as yet no image. Throughout the auditorium, hundreds of eager Wave members hunched forward in their seats, staring at the blank blue tubes and waiting.

Outside, David and Laurie tried a set of auditorium doors, but found them locked. They quickly tried a second set, but found those locked also. But there were more doors to try, and they ran around the side of the auditorium looking for them.

The television screens were still blank. No face appeared on the screen and no sounds came from the speakers. Around the auditorium students began to squirm and murmur with anxiety. Why wasn't anything happening? Where was their leader? What were they supposed to do? As the tension in the room continued to build, the same question passed through their minds over and over: what were they supposed to do?

From the side of the stage, Ben looked down at them, as the sea of faces stared back at him anxiously. Was it really true that the natural inclination of people was to look for a leader? Someone to make decisions for them? Indeed, the faces looking up at him said it was. That was the awesome responsibility any leader had, knowing that a group like this would follow. Ben began to realize how much more serious this 'little experiment' was than he'd ever imagined. It was frightening how easily they would put their faith in your hands, how easily they would let you decide for them. If people were destined to be led, Ben thought, this was something he must make sure they learned: to question thoroughly, never to put your faith in anyone's hands blindly. Otherwise . . .

From the centre of the audience a single frustrated student suddenly jumped up from his seat and shouted at Mr Ross, 'There is no leader, is there!'

Shocked students around the auditorium quickly turned as two Wave guards rushed the offender out of the auditorium. In the confusion that followed, Laurie and David were able to slip in through the door the guards had opened.

Before the students had time to think about what had just happened, Ben strode to the centre of the auditorium stage again. 'Yes, you have a leader!' he shouted. That was the cue Carl Block had been waiting for as he hid backstage. Now he pulled back the stage curtains to reveal a large movie screen. At the same moment, Alex Cooper, in the projection room, flicked on a projector.

'There!' Ben shouted at the auditorium full of students. 'There is your leader!'

The auditorium was filled with gasps and exclamations of surprise as the gigantic image of Adolf Hitler appeared on the screen.

'That's it!' Laurie whispered excitedly to David. 'That's the movie he showed us that day!'

'Now listen carefully!' Ben shouted at them. 'There is no National Wave Youth Movement. There is no leader. But if there was, *he* would have been it. Do you see what you've become? Do you see where you were headed? How far would you have gone? Take a look at your future!'

The film left Adolf Hitler and focused on the faces of the young Nazis who fought for him during World War Two. Many of them were only teenagers, some even younger than the students in the audience.

'You thought you were so special!' Ross told them. 'Better than everyone outside this room. You traded your freedom for what you said was equality. But you turned your equality into superiority over non-Wave members. You accepted the group's will over your own convictions, no matter who you had to hurt to do it. Oh, some of you thought you were just going along for the ride, that you could walk away at any moment. But did you? Did any of you try it?

'Yes, you all would have made good Nazis,' Ben told them. 'You would have put on the uniforms, turned your heads, and allowed your friends and neighbours to be persecuted and destroyed. You say it could never happen again, but look how close you came. Threatening those who wouldn't join you, preventing non-Wave members from sitting with you at football games. Fascism isn't something those other people did, it is right here, in all of us. You ask how could the German people do nothing as millions of innocent human beings were murdered? How could they claim they weren't involved? What causes people to deny their own histories?'

Ben moved closer to the front of the stage and spoke in a lower voice: 'If history repeats itself, you will all want to deny what happened to you in The Wave. But, if our experiment has been successful – and I think you can see that it has – you will have learned that we are all responsible for our own actions, and that you must always question what you do rather than blindly follow a leader, and that for the rest of your lives, you will never, ever allow a group's will to usurp your individual rights.'

Ben paused for a moment. So far he'd made it sound like they were all at fault. But it was more than that. 'Now listen to me, please,' he said. 'I owe you an apology. I know this has been painful to you. But in a way it could be argued that none of you are as at fault as I am for leading you to this. I meant The Wave to be a great lesson for you and perhaps I succeeded too well. I certainly became more of a leader than I intended to be. And I hope you will believe me when I say that it has been a painful lesson for me too. All I can add is, I hope this is a lesson we'll all share for the rest of our lives. If we're smart, we won't dare forget it.'

The effect on the students was staggering. All around the auditorium they were slowly rising from their seats. A few were in tears, others tried to avoid the eyes of those next to them. All looked stunned by the lesson they had learned. As they left they discarded their posters and banners. The floor quickly became littered with yellow membership cards and all thoughts of military posture were forgotten as they slunk out of the auditorium.

Laurie and David walked slowly down the aisle, passing the sombre students filing out of the room. Amy was coming towards them, her head bowed. When she looked up and saw Laurie she burst into tears and ran to hug her friend.

Behind her, David saw Eric and Brian. Both looked shaken. They stopped when they saw David and for a few moments the three team-mates stood in an awkward silence.

'What a freak-out,' Eric said, his voice hardly more than a mumble.

David tried to shrug it off. He felt bad for his friends. 'Well, it's over now,' he told them. 'Let's try and forget it . . . I mean, let's try not to forget it . . . but let's forget it at the same time.'

Eric and Brian nodded. They understood what he meant even if he hadn't exactly made sense.

Brian made a rueful face. 'I should've known it,' he said. 'The first time that Clarkstown linebacker broke through and sacked me for a fifteen-yard loss last Saturday. I should've known it was no good.'

The three team-mates shared a short chuckle and then Eric and Brian left the auditorium. David walked down towards the stage where Mr Ross stood. His teacher looked very tired.

'I'm sorry I didn't trust you, Mr Ross,' David said.

'No, it was good that you didn't,' Ross told him. 'You showed good judgement. I should be apologizing to you, David. I should have told you what I was planning to do.'

Laurie joined them. 'Mr Ross, what's going to happen now?' she asked.

Ben shrugged and shook his head. 'I'm not sure I know, Laurie. We still have quite a bit of history to cover this semester. But maybe we'll take just one more period to discuss what happened today.'

'I think we should,' David said.

'You know, Mr Ross,' Laurie said. 'In a way I'm glad this happened. I mean, I'm sorry it had to come to this, but I'm glad it worked out, and I think everyone learned a lot.'

Ben nodded. 'Well, that's nice of you, Laurie. But I've already decided this is one lesson I'm going to skip in next year's course.'

David and Laurie looked at each other and smiled. They said good-bye to Mr Ross and turned to leave the auditorium.

Ben watched Laurie and David and the last of the former members of The Wave leave the auditorium. When they were gone and he thought he was alone, he sighed and said, 'Thank God.' He was relieved that it had ended well, and thankful that he still had his job at Gordon High. There would still be a few angry parents and incensed faculty members to smooth over, but in time he knew he could do it.

He turned and was about to leave the stage when he heard a sob and saw Robert leaning against one of the television sets, tears running down his face.

Poor Robert, Ben thought. The only one who really stood to lose in this whole thing. He walked towards the trembling student and put his arm around his shoulder. 'You know, Robert,' he said, trying to cheer him up, 'you look good in a tie and jacket. You ought to wear them more often.'

Through his tears, Robert managed a smile. 'Thanks, Mr Ross.'

'What do you say we go out for a bite to eat?' Ben said, leading him off the stage. 'There are some things I think we should talk about.'

Afterword

The Wave is based on a true incident that occurred in a high school history class in Palo Alto, California, in 1969. For three years afterwards, according to the teacher, Ron Jones, no one talked about it. 'It was,' he said, 'one of the most frightening events I have ever experienced in the classroom.'

'The Wave' disrupted an entire school. The novel dramatizes the incident, showing how the powerful forces of group pressure that have pervaded many historical movements and cults can persuade people to join such movements and give up their individual rights in the process – sometimes causing great harm to others. The full impact on the students of what they lived through and learned is realistically portrayed in the book.

In addition to the novel, *The Wave* has been made into a one-hour television show for ABC by Virginia L. Carter, an executive director at Tandem Productions and T.A.T. Communications Company.

HARRIET HARVEY COFFIN
Project Consultant
T.A.T. Communications Company

www.puffin.co.uk.www.puffin.co.uk.www.puffin.co.uk
ookinfo.competitions.news.games.sneakpreviews
www.puffin.co.uk.www.puffin.co.uk.www.puffin.co.uk
dventure.bestsellers.fun.coollinks.freestuff
www.puffin.co.uk.www.puffin.co.uk.www.puffin.co.uk
xplore.yourshout.awards.toptips.authorinfo
www.puffin.co.uk.www.puffin.co.uk.www.puffin.co.uk
reatbooks.greatbooks.greatbooks.greatbooks
www.puffin.co.uk.www.puffin.co.uk.www.puffin.co.uk
eviews.poems.jokes.authorevents.audioclips
www.puffin.co.uk.www.puffin.co.uk.www.puffin.co.uk
terviews.e-mailupdates.bookinfo.competitions.news

www.puffin.co.uk

ames.sneakpreviews.adventure.bestsellers.fun
www.puffin.co.uk.www.puffin.co.uk.www.puffin.co.uk
ookinfo.competitions.news.games.sneakpreviews
www.puffin.co.uk.www.puffin.co.uk.www.puffin.co.uk
dventure.bestsellers.fun.coollinks.freestuff
www.puffin.co.uk.www.puffin.co.uk.www.puffin.co.uk
xplore.yourshout.awards.toptips.authorinfo
www.puffin.co.uk.www.puffin.co.uk.www.puffin.co.uk
reatbooks.greatbooks.greatbooks.greatbooks
www.puffin.co.uk.www.puffin.co.uk.www.puffin.co.uk
eviews.poems.jokes.authorevents.audioclips
www.puffin.co.uk.www.puffin.co.uk.www.puffin.co.uk

Read more in Puffin

For complete information about books available from Puffin – and Penguin – and how to order them, contact us at the appropriate address below. Please note that for copyright reasons the selection of books varies from country to country.

www.puffin.co.uk

In the United Kingdom: Please write to Dept EP, Penguin Books Ltd, Bath Road, Harmondsworth, West Drayton, Middlesex UB7 ODA

In the United States: Please write to Penguin Putnam Inc., P.O. Box 12289, Dept B, Newark, New Jersey 07101–5289 or call 1–800–788–6262

In Canada: Please write to Penguin Books Canada Ltd, 10 Alcorn Avenue, Suite 300, Toronto, Ontario M4V 3B2

In Australia: Please write to Penguin Books Australia Ltd, P.O. Box 257, Ringwood, Victoria 3134

In New Zealand: Please write to Penguin Books (NZ) Ltd, Private Bag 102902, North Shore Mail Centre, Auckland 10

In India: Please write to Penguin Books India Pvt Ltd, 11 Panscheel Shopping Centre, Panscheel Park, New Delhi 110 017

In the Netherlands: Please write to Penguin Books Netherlands bv, Postbus 3507, NL–1001 AH Amsterdam

In Germany: Please write to Penguin Books Deutschland GmbH, Metzlerstrasse 26, 60594 Frankfurt am Main

In Spain: Please write to Penguin Books S. A., Bravo Murillo 19, 1° B, 28015 Madrid

In Italy: Please write to Penguin Italia s.r.l., Via Felice Casati 20, I–20124 Milano

In France: Please write to Penguin France S. A., 17 rue Lejeune, F–31000 Toulouse

In Japan: Please write to Penguin Books Japan, Ishikiribashi Building, 2–5–4, Suido, Bunkyo-ku, Tokyo 112

In South Africa: Please write to Longman Penguin Southern Africa (Pty) Ltd, Private Bag X08, Bertsham 2013